CERATOSAURUS

A NOVEL BY MICHAEL COLE

SEVEREDPRESS

CERATOSAURUS

WWW.SEVEREDPRESS.COM

ISBN: 978-1-923663-13-8

CERATOSAURUS

A NOVEL BY MICHAEL COLE

www.severedpress.com

CHAPTER 1

"Let me in! It's getting through the glass! Let me in!"

Zimo kept his back to the storage room door. For the last seven years, he considered Rong a good friend, and himself to be a man who would do anything for his friends. The truth of that self-perception had forever changed, for fear was a powerful drug.

Their jobs in this little fortress were simple ones. They were the cooks, just one up from being at the bottom of the totem pole. Janitors were considered the lowest. The culture of this business gave status to the administrative and scientific staff members. They were considered the most important and irreplaceable. The rest of the staff hardly understood what the project was even about. Zimo and Rong weren't even sure exactly what was being stored in the main building. They just knew it was of immense importance.

They almost never got out of the mess hall. There was always work to be done and no time for recreation. What little downtime they had was spent in the staff lounge, playing cards with some of the maintenance workers. Only a few times did they even get to step outside and get a glance at the science facility. It resembled a large barn, barricaded from the rest of the compound by a large wire fence. According to one of the maintenance guys, somewhere in the back was a large paddock, where nobody except a few key personnel had access to.

At one point, they learned two things. The project involved some sort of animals. And some of them were *big*. Even then, the scientists and administration didn't consider it worthwhile enough to inform the lower-level staff of the nature of the project.

"Just focus on your job," they always said.

As it turned out, those 'important' science personnel were the first to die. Next were the administrative staff and most of the security officers, all in a span of minutes.

The evacuation effort was short-lived, Zimo was told by Rong before they were ambushed. He didn't see it for himself, but he heard the stomps from the big one and a massive explosion. Given the smell of burnt fuel, it was safe to assume the personnel carrier had crashed and ruptured its fuel tank.

The creatures did not care about class distinction. As far as they were concerned, all human meat tasted the same. Now, they were on a search and destroy mission for anyone that was left.

Zimo's heart raced. The door shuddered against his back as Rong tried to force his way into the storage room.

"Let me in, damn it!"

Zimo heard the shattering of the glass window separating the kitchen from the mess hall. There was a hair-raising screeching noise of a creature hellbent on killing. Next came a frightened scream and a final shake of the door.

"Zimo, please!!! NOOO!!!!"

The shake was punctuated with a heavy *thud* as he was slammed against the door.

Zimo jumped away, listening to the grotesque sounds of fabric and flesh being torn and the gagging noise of blood being vomited. He backed to the rear of the storage room, all at once ashamed of his cowardice, while hoping the beast would be satisfied gorging on his friend.

Several pots, pans, and utensils were smacked from the countertops and walls by its slashing tail. It made a ravenous growl as it attacked, as if it was determined to strike fear into the heart of its victim up to the moment of death. Or maybe it was for anyone and everyone nearby, warning them that they were next.

One thing was clear—these things were not just killing for food. Sure, they were carnivores and would be gorging for a while, due to the abundance of bodies. But, judging by the way they went after everyone, they were acting out of pure hatred.

He held his breath and remained perfectly still, not daring to make even a hint of a sound. Maybe the thing would go away after it was done with Rong. The man he had known for several years and had worked alongside with nonstop for the past six months was nothing more than an asset now. Just a dish to tide the beast over.

The growling stopped.

Large feet, tipped with twelve-inch claws, hit the floor. Each footstep was an epicenter for rippling vibrations which made their way to the terrified Zimo.

It stopped.

Next, Zimo heard sniffing. It studied the wall in the same manner a canine would, only this one was large enough to touch the ceiling.

More footsteps thumped against the floor, each one growing more distant.

Zimo gently exhaled. It was moving away. Maybe it was satisfied. Maybe it and the others would go away, and grant him an opportunity to get to one of the boats and evacuate.

An ear-piercing roar made him jump. Next came rapid footsteps, rapidly getting louder and nearer.

Stomp! Stomp! Stomp! Stomp! Stomp! Stomp! Stomp!

SMASH!!!

The door exploded into a hundred pieces. In its place was the large head of one of the juveniles. Even through the fright and dust, Zimo saw its orange eyes and the red horn on its nose. Its jaw was agape, showing off its many teeth and the evidence of previous victims stuck between them.

Zimo's reactionary motions caught its attention. It initiated a second charge, ramming through two rows of shelves like a rhinoceros. Boxes of canned products, flour, and vegetables were tossed every which way, along with the fragments of the shelving units.

The blockade of supplies granted Zimo a moment to make an escape. To his right was a door which led to the freezer unit. Where he would go from there, he had no idea. Nor did he care right now. He just needed to get the hell out of here!

He ran through the door, slammed it shut, and twisted the lock.

Even with the rush of adrenaline and the heart-gripping fright, Zimo took notice of the sunshine beaming down on him. The freezer was anything but cold. That, and there was wind brushing against his back.

He turned around and gazed into what used to be the freezer room. The back wall had been smashed in completely, resulting in ceiling collapse.

When the attack first occurred, he and Rong initially hid in the kitchen. There, they thought they heard a thunderous boom coming from this area, but weren't sure what to make of it. In the tense minutes that followed, they quickly forgot about it and focused on preserving their own lives.

Now, it was obvious. The big one had been here.

He could hear its thunderous footsteps somewhere to the west. Rifle shots rang out in that same direction. One of the security guys must have survived the initial slaughter.

The footsteps intensified and a deep roar pierced the afternoon sky. The gunman let out a brief scream. Next came a *CHOMP!* like a conclusive drumbeat, and the trickling of blood against the ground.

Zimo stepped over the rubble and took a glance to the eastern part of the compound. The garage was destroyed, as were two of the personnel trailers. Only one remained intact.

He cringed after seeing movement in his peripheral vision.

It was Shui, one of the maintenance staff members. He was running from the west, probably having witnessed the demise of the last security guard.

The sight of another living human was a welcome one. Better yet, it wasn't just some random worker, but somebody who was a good buddy of Zimo's. They played cards together in the evenings and told stories about their family life back home.

By the looks of it, Shui had the same idea as Zimo. He was going right for the trailer.

Zimo opened his mouth to call to him, only to be cut off by an impact against the freezer door. He glanced over his shoulder, just in time to see the second hit. This one successfully detached the door from its hinges, allowing the carnivore to squeeze through the frame.

Shrieking, Zimo sprinted for the trailer.

Shui was standing in its entryway, now looking in his direction after hearing the crashing noise.

"Hold the door open! Wait for me! Wait for me! Wait for me!" Zimo cried.

Heavy footsteps alerted him to the monster's rapid approach. He kept his eyes on the trailer. He was almost there! Just a few more steps, and he would be inside.

Shui was wide-eyed and pissing his pants.

"Keep it open!" Zimo said.

The door slammed shut and the lock twisted into place.

Zimo threw himself against the door and tried in vain to turn the handle. Shui, a friend—a man who shared photos of his two-year-old daughter every night—now saw him as nothing more than an asset. Bait to hopefully satisfy the beast and prolong his own survival.

Those footsteps closed in. Hot breath touched his neck as the gargantuan shadow encompassed him.

"NOOO!!!"

Crushing bite pressure crushed his shoulder, driving knife-like teeth deep into his flesh. He was lifted off the ground and shaken.

All Zimo could do was kick his legs and scream, then grunt after the beast threw him to the ground. The impact resulted in four broken limbs and a concussion, nearly resulting in loss of consciousness.

The haziness did not obscure the agony of what came next.

Zimo felt the thing's snout roll him onto his back. Next, those jaws tore into the soft flesh of his belly.

He was back to screaming.

His last sight was that of his intestines being lifted from his abdomen. Behind the bloody curtain was the trailer. On the other side of its window was a frightened Shui, who quickly pulled a curtain between him and the horror, hoping the creature would remain ignorant of his presence.

CHAPTER 2

THREE MONTHS LATER

Claude Van lit his cigarette and listened to the surf washing ashore. He couldn't see the beach through the hills and trees, but it was close. Temptingly close. Sitting on that sand sounded better than standing guard against literally nothing.

They were on a small island. Their main operation wasn't even here, but over on King's Chamber, just over a mile northwest. It was only due to their leader's insistence that they conduct a dig on this little neighboring piece of land just outside of the South China Sea. Why not unearth a hidden stockpile of weapons abandoned by the PLA while retrieving resources from an abandoned research project? It would come in handy for the next job. Knowing their leader, there was much work to be done. Embassies to bomb, terror groups to finance, regimes to topple, countries to destabilize. Anything to weaken the influence of the West and gain power.

He took a moment to peek into the camp. Six tents surrounded the dig site. Without heavy machinery, the men had to work by the sweat of their brow.

The job was overseen by Torrez. Second-in-command of their independent regiment, he was as cold-blooded and as much of an idealist as their leader, Zahara. It was precisely why he was put in charge of operations when the boss was not available.

It wasn't often they did a job like this. Zahara preferred to answer to nobody. He was his own man with his own agenda. But agendas required finances and resources. Their client provided both.

The money was good and the job was relatively easy: obtain a bunch of high-tech, experimental science bullshit from some abandoned lab. Not complicated at all. They just needed to beat everyone else to the punch.

Claude went to draw from his cigarette when he heard approaching footsteps. He lifted his AK-47, only to immediately lower it after recognizing Burchette emerging from the forest. The island's vegetation wasn't excessively thick. It wasn't the Amazon or some of the islands near Japan. But there were enough obstructions to make a man nervous.

Burchette glanced over his shoulder a couple of times as he approached. His hands, tattooed during years of affiliation with a number of terror groups, gripped his rifle tightly.

"Careful there," Claude said. "You'll shoot your own foot off."

Burchette kept watching the distance. "Shh."

Claude listened and watched the forest. After several moments, he glared at his fellow guard.

"There's nothing there. What's got you so wound up?"

"Thought I heard a chopper some time ago," Burchette said. He sat next to Claude and snatched a cigarette from his shirt pocket. He lit it and took a long draw.

"Probably just some naval patrol. Not too uncommon for them to operate around here. They have no reason to investigate us. Hardly anyone knows we're here."

The statement nearly made Burchette choke on his cigarette. "Listen here, idiot. There's always eyes on us. Always. Someone, somewhere, knows where we are. No matter where we are, no matter where we go."

Claude sniggered and finished off his own cigarette. "Whatever you say. Nobody's interested in this little island chain."

"That's because hardly anyone knows what Zahara is looking for," Burchette said. "There's a reason the project is top secret. Hell, we don't even know exactly what it is we're transporting. We're just hired to slip into Chinese territory, retrieve the whatever-it-is, and bug out. And do it without getting caught."

"You said earlier the PLA abandoned this place. Why would they care if we're here?"

"It's not them I'm worried about," Burchette replied. He took another look around. "Like I said, always assume there's eyes on us."

Claude chuckled at his paranoid comrade. He stood up and mocked Burchette's insistent watch of the forest.

"Oh, man. I can sense it. Someone's out there."

Burchette sneered. "You think you're funny?"

Claude sported a grin. "I think I am." He aimed his AK-47 into the trees. "I know you're out there. You're not fooling me—"

WHOOSH!

Claude tried to suck in a breath, but only took in a river of his own blood. He dropped his rifle and fell to his knees, hand clutching the handle of the knife embedded in his throat.

It had come out of nowhere, appearing as tiny as a mosquito in the initial split-second it emerged from the depths of the forest. Only when its blade sunk four inches into his neck did he finally come to understand Burchette's warning.

As it turned out, even *he* was caught off guard.

Right after Claude's knees hit the ground, a dark figure emerged from the forest. Somehow, someway, this intruder managed to inch his way toward their post without being spotted. He had a knife in hand and buried all six inches of its blade into Burchette's neck.

He watched his partner's corpse faceplant into the dirt. Next, the curtains closed in and his brain shut down. His final sensation was one of falling forward.

As soon as the body hit the dirt, Elliot Kittner crouched and unslung his rifle. After confirming his position remained uncompromised, he faced the jungle and signaled for his squad to approach.

Silent as ghosts, the team of mercenaries assembled near their commander. At the front of the group was Herschel Engel, a man straight out of the Bronx, who brought a fighting spirit carried since birth. No longer was he a street brawler, but a trained killer who wielded a discipline rivaling that of Shaolin monks.

Behind Herschel was Tajima, a descendent of a Pearl Harbor bomber, seeking to reclaim honor to the family name by serving for good ol' Uncle Sam. After eight years of Army service, he decided he was ready to make real money in the private sector.

Roach crouched beside the imperial descendant. Like Tajima, he came from a long line of dishonor. His father was a career criminal, serving in the Cartel south of the Rio Grande, like his father before him. Unlike Tajima, Roach was not interested in restoring honor. He simply found this kind of work much more interesting. Morals aside, Kittner knew him to be reliable and loyal.

In this business, those were two essential traits.

Kittner whispered into his radio, "Team One in position. Two and Three, update when ready."

A moment passed before Metwally's growly voice came through his earpiece. *"Team Two, in position. Sentries on north side have been dispatched."*

Next came Costa's voice. *"Team Three in position. Watch units on the west dispatched. Perimeter secured. Awaiting instructions."*

"Stand by."

Kittner gently peeked over the mound to get a look at the camp. There were six tents surrounding a small depression. Working throughout were a little over two-dozen of Zahara's minions. They referred to themselves as specters; spirits in the night, striking unexpectedly and inflicting fear onto the world.

Kittner knew the truth. They were nothing more than barbaric, low-rent henchmen, picked because of ideology, willingness to work cheap, and their lack of regard for innocent lives. Only a couple of figures in this group of self-described specters had any notoriety.

One of those was the head of their organization.

Zahara was the only name he was known by. For many years, he was considered a second-rate terrorist. Just some asshole who blew things up and considered himself important. But after the bombing of a French embassy in Libya, his notoriety drastically increased. Rumors spread of him potentially being a CIA informant, which enabled him to avoid military retaliation by the United States.

It would not be his first run-in with these bastards. That was in the Bialowieza Forest between Belarus and Poland. It was there Kittner was first given the assignment to intercept an associate of Zahara's, who was believed to be prepping a chemical attack on the Polish capital.

With intel informing him of a small encampment, Kittner led a four-man team into the forest. He found the target and eliminated him. Unfortunately, at that time, Zahara was present with a team of specters.

The terrorist leader, smiling with his deformed lower lip, separated Kittner's good friend, Jason Hall, from the camp and executed him with a shot to the head.

Kittner rarely held grudges. This one was blood deep. When the call came from a wealthy client in Montana concerning an operation near the South China Sea, he jumped at the opportunity. Apparently, the client, nicknamed Sam Penyard—real names were rarely shared—had an interest in this island. Something had been left here by the Chinese, who were apparently in cahoots with a 'businessman' in the American Midwest. That businessman was a competitor to Sam Penyard, and he had hired a specific crew to retrieve some valuable goods from some goods in the Citadel Chain.

Whatever was here, it was worth a lot. Kittner could not care less what those 'goods' were. The only detail that interested him was the man believed to be running the operation.

That led him to now.

Kittner raised a pair of binoculars to his eyes and scoped the dig site out. There were several assault rifles present, mainly AK-47s. This was not a casual dig. They were excavating something worth killing for.

He panned the glasses right to study the north side. There were two guards seated, smoking cigarettes, watching their comrades do the hard labor. In the space between two tents six meters south of them was another pair tending to a campfire. Something was boiling in that pot. Regardless of his hatred for these men, Kittner could not deny that the stew, or whatever it was, smelled pretty damn good. If only these guys devoted their lives to something useful like cooking instead of terrorism.

Panning left to the south part of the camp, he spotted a man with a long, jagged scar in the middle of a huge bald spot on the right side of his head. He was a little under six feet and wore a constant snarl on his face.

His name was Torrez. Second-in-command of Zahara's operations, he was as respected and feared as the top dog by the lackeys. He was originally a drug runner for the Mexican Cartels, before eventually getting on the bad side of one of the drug lords. Realizing his time on this earth was limited if he remained near the Rio Grande, he decided to render his services across the globe. Somehow or another, he met Zahara. The rest was history—something Kittner intended to conclude.

"Who's on the roster, Chief?" Herschel asked.

Kittner sank next to the mound to speak with his men. "Don't have a visual on the target. Torrez is here, acting all high and mighty."

"Damn. Means the head honcho is somewhere else, then," Herschel replied.

"If we have to, we'll beat the information out of the bastard." Kittner unslung his HK416 rifle and prepared to scale the mound. After taking one last look at the camp, he leaned into his radio mic. "Team Two, hit the guards and the tent grouping. Check each target. It's possible our objective is present in the shelters near you. If not, we will aim to capture Torrez alive. Team Three, provide sniper support. They'll be pushed your way, so it'll be like shooting fish in a barrel. Grezda, do be sure not to send any bullets my way."

"Don't know what you're referring to, Chief..."

"Uh-huh." Kittner glanced at his fireteam. Using hand signals, he directed them to a six-meter spread. He climbed over the mound and crouched near a tree. "On my mark..."

A guard was walking along the inner perimeter. He was lost in thought, bored from repetitive walking and tired from his turn in the dig. He was only a few yards from Kittner.

The mercenary inched forward, knife in hand.

With a yawn, the sentry began to turn.

Kittner quickened his pace, remaining low to the ground, only extending to his full height when he reached the target. He cupped the man's mouth and ran the blade across his neck, nullifying his ability to alert the others.

He was inside the perimeter now, a mere few yards away from some specters seated near the southeast tent. A generator rumbled behind them, with a pair of fuel drums stationed right next to it. The rattling sound helped to obscure his presence as he inched closer.

Now two yards away from the seated men, he carefully unscrewed the cap on one of the drums. It was full to the top. He screwed the cap back on and lowered the drum onto its side.

There was a slight incline from here to the center of the camp. Just enough for the barrel to roll freely once given a good push.

Kittner had one thing to do first. He placed an incendiary charge on the drum and started a seven-second countdown.

A heavy kick sent the drum rolling past the seated men and into the interior of the camp. Several eyes turned toward the four-hundred-pound metal container. For some, it was the last thing they would see.

The charge exploded, turning the barrel into a fifteen-foot fireball. Its explosion rocked the camp, sending unsuspecting specters hurtling through the air, their bodies trailing smoke.

Men scattered. Some gathered weapons, others simply trying to distance themselves from the newly formed lake of flames. A few ran in circles, having been touched by the reach of the fiery tendrils.

In the midst of that chaos came one sign of order. Torrez turned his eyes to the direction where the fuel drum came from and beheld the sight of the six-foot-two man in black.

Pointing, he shouted his warning to the camp. By then, it didn't matter. The assault had started.

Kittner took aim with his HK416. The three men in front of him were in the middle of turning around to face him, AK-47s at their hips. A trio of three-round bursts tore their chests open and sent them reeling backwards, rifles firing uselessly into the sky.

The rest of Team One advanced. Herschel was three meters to Kittner's three o'clock, placing bullets into a tenacious terrorist who tried charging their position. A few others attempted to hold the line, but were quickly driven back by suppressing fire by Tajima and Roach.

Team Two, led by Metwally, launched their attack from the north. A few grenades burst near the four tents, shredding their tarps with shrapnel. Flustered gunmen attempted to repel them, but were quickly cut down to size, not just by the superior weaponry and tactics of Metwally's three-man fireteam, but the sniper fire coming in from the west.

One by one, specters started dropping out of nowhere, a puff of pink mist bursting from their exit wounds.

Kittner moved left around the southeast tent. A gunman appeared from around the corner, intending to intercept him, only to take three shots to the torso. As he fell backward, another one tried to take cover from behind a chest full of equipment. He fired a few shots in the direction of Team One, failing to hit a single intruder.

Herschel beat Kittner to the punch this time, cracking the gunman's skull with a well-placed shot above the left eye.

To the north, members of this encampment were dropping like flies. Those who managed to take cover from the onslaught from Teams One and Two were picked off by the snipers Grezda and Donovan.

Kittner's focus went to the southern part of the camp. Torrez and two of his subordinates were making a run for it, leaving his dwindling defenders to hold off the attacking group with their lives.

"We've got runners. I'm on 'em."

With his team finishing off the rest of the encampment, Kittner sprinted south. He passed through several yards of vegetation, the targets up ahead by a few meters.

One of them, sensing their pursuer, decided to try and hold his ground. Pivoting on his heel, the man opened fire in Kittner's direction. His aim was off, planting rounds several inches to the mercenary's left shoulder.

Kittner's aim, on the other hand, was on point. Three pink clouds ruptured from the target's back. Arms outstretched and eyes wide in shock, he fell backward.

Kittner resumed the chase. Torrez and his companion were maybe sixty feet ahead of him. Their intent was clear; a dock had been constructed on the south shore. Torrez was attempting to make a fast getaway.

The canopy began to thin. They were nearing the beach.

Kittner ran as fast as he could, but could not seem to close the distance. He could not afford to lose the son of a bitch.

"Chamberlain!" he spoke into his mouthpiece. "Get your ass to the south shore. Torrez is making a run for it."

"Swinging around, Chief."

He could hear rotor blades somewhere to his right. Next, he heard machine-gun fire.

Kittner reached the beach just in time to see Torrez's associate get torn in half by the Sikorsky UH-60 Blackhawk's M240 machine guns.

Torrez turned back, abandoning the large cruiser in favor of the cover naturally provided by the island's interior. After two steps, he stopped again, seeing Kittner closing in on him.

Kittner knew the deal. He wanted Torrez alive, and the bastard was not going to give himself up willingly, not even under these circumstances. In a sprint, he charged the terrorist, knocking him backward with a kick to the chest.

Torrez fell on his back, his AK-47 flying from his grasp. His attempt to right himself was cut short by a strike to the forehead with the butt of Kittner's rifle. The terrorist sprawled out on the sand, unconscious.

Kittner caught his breath and waved to the chopper pilot. He could see Chamberlain through the glass window, replying with a thumbs up.

"Package is secure. Herschel, how are things back at camp?" he asked.

"All hostiles neutralized. Area is secure."

"Good. Join me at the south beach. Once Torrez awakens from his beauty sleep, we're going to have a friendly chat."

"You got it, boss. We're heading your way."

There was an eagerness in his voice. Everyone knew this 'chit-chat' would be anything but friendly. A bastard like Torrez deserved every second of what was coming.

CHAPTER 3

A gentle surf lapped onto the warm sand, providing a wake-up tap to the two souls laying face-down among scattered wreckage. The sun-warmed saltwater repeatedly stretched up the length of Sadie Calis' body, reminding her she had survived the nightmare that besieged her charter that early morning.

She registered the sensation of wet sand under her palms and face, and the hammering of hot sunlight from the sky. Judging from its position, it was close to noon. Fighting against grogginess, Sadie lifted her head. Clumps of sand clung to her long, brown hair, seemingly attempting to weigh her down. Her muscles ached, both from hours of swimming and dehydration.

For a moment, she succumbed to her feebleness and lay her head in the sand. The sound of the ocean brushing over the shore was soothing. Though only for a few moments.

Her mind transformed sounds of gentle surf into huge thrashing waves, blended with sounds of a cracking hull, shattering glass, groaning metal, and Lewy's voice barking instructions at her.

Flashes of the horrendous encounter served as a defibrillator to her system. With a shriek, Sadie Calis pushed herself off the beach and turned around. She was fully awake now, her survival tendencies overriding the strain of dehydration and exhaustion.

Standing in the sunlight, she watched the ocean. Finally, it registered. She had washed ashore on an island. One of the islands of the Citadel Chain, to be precise. Sadie only knew that because that was her destination. She wasn't expecting the voyage to be a luxury cruise. In fact, she even anticipated trouble. It was all part of the territory of investigative reporting.

But there was no way she could have anticipated *that.*

They were nearing the island when the monstrosity rose from the ocean. Limbs towered over the yacht, soulless and without compassion. They sought only to destroy.

And destroy, they did, and with great ease. The aftermath of their wrath lay in the sand, surrounding Lewy's unconscious body.

"Lewy!" she exclaimed. Sadie ran to his side and shook him by the shoulders. "Lewy? You alright?"

The forty-eight-year-old Australian yachtsman groaned. He raised his head, undergoing the same wake-up process his client had gone through a minute prior. Pushing himself onto his hands and knees, he evaluated his surroundings.

"Well, look at that. We're alive."

"For now," Sadie said.

Lewy stood up and stretched. "Considering what we just went through, I'll consider that a win." His enthusiasm dwindled after gazing upon the wreckage of his yacht. "Had that boat for eleven years. It's the one thing I kept in the divorce. When I said yes to the crazy investigative reporter making crazy claims about land being sold off, I didn't realize I'd be visiting Jules Verne's Mysterious Island."

"Listen, I had no idea *that* was going to happen." Sadie wrapped her arms around herself, thinking of the horrific attack. "What was that thing?"

"How should I know?" Lewy said. "This adventure was your endeavor. I just supplied the ride."

"But you've sailed around here before, haven't you?"

"From time to time, yes," Lewy said.

"And you've never seen anything like that?"

Lewy's brow wrinkled. "If I had, don't you think it would've come up during our meeting?"

Sadie shrugged. The man had a point. She turned and looked at the island's interior. Plenty of mangroves and other lush, green plants obscured her line of sight.

Lewy was busy sorting through the wreckage. He walked a hundred paces up the beach before exclaiming "ah-ha!" and sprinting into the water. Sadie walked in his direction, momentarily thinking the man had lost his mind, until he grabbed something out of the water and returned to shore.

In his hands was a small survival kit.

"Managed to get this out of the wheelhouse before the yacht went down," he said. He placed the small, waterproof box on the sand and opened it. Inside were freeze-dried foods and packs of water. He tossed one to Sadie, who immediately opened the pouch and sent its contents to the back of her throat.

She took a breath, her throat already feeling better.

"How long will this last us?" she asked.

"About a week," he replied. "Comes with a little life tent. We'll set it up later if we don't find a cave or something to hide in."

"If we are where I think we are, there might already be shelter," Sadie said.

Lewy took a glance at the beach and gave thought to their coordinates before the attack on their boat.

"Definitely in the Citadel Chain," he said. He backed up to the waterline to get the best view he could. He determined which way was north and tried to get an idea of the island's shape. "Looks like there's some elevation on the northwest side. There's a peninsula over that way, on the southwest corner. I say we've arrived on King's Chamber."

It was the main island in the chain, and the very place Sadie wanted to visit. Granted, she didn't expect such a hostile welcome.

More images of those huge, leathery arms crept into her subconscious. It was an impossible sight, one she could not believe she had experienced, let alone survived.

"I don't suppose you have a satellite phone or GPS tracker in that pack," she said.

"Yes, and yes," Lewy said. "I just need to dig through all of this stuff and find them. After that, we'll just need to sit tight for, I don't know, a day or two before someone comes along. Might be best for us to stay here at the beach." He sifted through some items and located the phone and tracker. "Hallelujah! All I need to do is switch this on, and we are set to go…"

BANG!

The tracker 'jumped' out of his grasp and broke into a dozen pieces. Lewy and Sadie jumped back, recognizing the burst of noise as a pistol shot. They turned to look at the tree line as a small band of men dressed in ragged paramilitary gear stepped into the open.

They were unkempt, dirty, tired, and above all, sinister. They held assault rifles and each had a sidearm strapped to their hip or leg.

Sadie's heart jumped into her throat. Her first thought was of pirates. Being a woman, there was a natural fear that came from being captured by such fiends. Generally, these types were not content with just thievery. Lacking any sense of morals, they took what they wanted, whether it was material goods or 'other' pleasures.

The man in the lead stood just under six feet. He had four days of growth on his face, the dark hairs of his youth fading with patches of grey. Wrinkles and marks decorated his skin. It was not age brought upon by many decades of living—in fact, Sadie pegged the man for somewhere in his forties—but from constant stress and hatred.

His companions were not much better. Sadie counted seven of them, and all of them looked as though they had seen better days.

The man in charge kept his pistol pointed at Lewy. He eyeballed their attire and equipment.

"Not many people come to this island."

To Sadie's surprise, he spoke with a South African accent. Her instinct placed him as Middle Eastern. Perhaps he was a mix. Looking at his men, she realized this wasn't a group from any one region of the globe. There was an Asian, a couple of Middle Eastern men, a Caucasian, and a Latino individual. It was essentially the French Foreign Legion of piracy.

Wherever they were from, they became something less than respectable.

"Listen, we're shipwrecked," Lewy said. He kept his hands raised and did not move a muscle.

"Is that right?" the leader said. "And you just so happened to come into the Citadel." He glanced at the camera hanging from Sadie's neck. "Just sightseeing, am I right?"

Lewy shrugged. "She is. I was just the charter. Frankly, I should've charged her a higher insurance fee." He sniggered at his own joke, hoping to alleviate the situation.

The man, looking at the wreckage lining the shore, cracked a smile. For a moment, he was laughing along with Lewy. His men joined in.

"I like this guy," one of them said.

Then, in the blink of an eye, the laughter stopped.

The man marched toward Sadie and dug his hand into her shirt and pants pockets. She kept perfectly still. It was clear he was looking for identification. For better or worse, she had left it in her cabin. During the sinking, she managed to grab her camera and film, but not her passport and wallet.

"I'm a journalist," she said.

"Are you now?" the man said. He stepped back and eyed her from head to toe. "For whom?"

"Independent."

She hated herself for giving that answer, even though it was the truth. It was evident this guy was paranoid. As he pointed out, not many people visited this stretch of land. Her very presence and the timing of it screamed she was an agent of some sort sent to track him.

The man's next move confirmed that mindset. He pointed the pistol at her forehead and held it there.

"Who sent you?"

"N-nobody. I'm here on my own," she said. She was fighting back tears at this point. Hours ago, she survived a horrific encounter with some enormously large beast that wrecked her ship, only to potentially get a bullet between the eyes.

The man kept the weapon fixed on her for what felt like forever. It twitched as his finger gently applied pressure on the trigger. The guy was probably figuring it was better to shoot her right here and alleviate his fears.

Time seemed to stop moving. Sadie closed her eyes, commended her soul, and waited for the loud crack of thunder.

The pistol lowered. She opened her eyes in time to see two of the gunmen approach. They took her by the arms and led her to the jungle.

"Take both of them," he said. "We'll figure out the truth soon enough."

“Wait, wait…” Lewy groaned as one of the men took his SAT phone and tossed it into the water. They grabbed him by the shirt and forced him into the interior of the island.

The two shipwreck survivors walked side by side eastward into the island, now prisoners of this unnamed crew of bandits.

The leader used his AK-47 to goad them in the back. “Keep moving.” He looked over his shoulder at one of his men. “Get ahold of Jarran’s team. I want them to take the two shrimp boats over to Sulfur Shores. Figure out what’s going on with Torrez’s group. They haven’t been responding to our radio calls.” “As you wish,” the associate said. “You think they’ve run into trouble?”

“Given the fact that more people than we thought are aware of the things taking place in this island chain, yeah, I think there’s reason to be concerned. There’s no reason for Torrez to be ignoring our calls. They should have the bombs and chemicals dug up by now.”

“Bombs and chemicals?” Sadie looked back at him. “Who are you?”

“Stop talking,” Lewy said.

They continued for several paces before Sadie leaned toward him. “You know who he is?”

He nodded, and whispered, “You heard of the French Embassy bombing?”

That was all she needed to know. Right then, it all came together. She knew there was a slight familiarity to the man’s face. He was not a pirate, but a terrorist.

His name was Zahara.

CHAPTER 4

Elliot Kittner tightened the restraints around Torrez's wrists and ankles, then smacked him twice across the face. The terrorist was slowly stirring from his brief slumber.

The snapping of a few twigs made the Master Chief look into the jungle.

"It's Herschel, sir. We're coming out."

His second-in-command emerged from the tree line, with Tajima and Roach right behind him.

"Excellent," Roach said. He placed his hand on his knife. "Want me to make the bastard talk?"

Kittner was tempted to take him up on that. "Let's see how this plays out."

A few moments later, Metwally, Alston, and Sorenson stepped out. Metwally, often referred to as the hillbilly of the team, had a thick beard and a layer of pudge on what used to be a finely trimmed six-pack. As active as the guy was, he typically maintained a poor diet. It was not so much a question of age, but discipline in his everyday life. Fortunately for the team, it was not anything that hindered his efficiency on the field, and that was the only thing that mattered to Kittner.

Alston and Sorenson were cousins from Harlem. Disinterested in continuing their family's electronics business, they decided to join the Marines, took part in missions in Bosnia and Iraq, and like many veterans, learned they could use their skillsets to make real cash. The two men were inseparable, their bond signified by a tattoo of a skull and pistol grip on their right forearms.

"Nice work, Chief," Sorenson said. "Guy's lucky I wasn't the one who got ahold of him. He'd be a lot less pretty."

"Still be better looking than you," Alston said.

"Shut up!"

Alston chuckled. "Not only that, but Torrez probably would've kicked *your* ass."

The other men chuckled at Sorenson's expense.

"Alright, knock it off," Kittner said. "Where the hell is Team Three?"

"Coming out," Costa announced. Walking alongside her sniper teammates, Donovan and Grezda, she arrived at the beach. She dabbed a handkerchief under her helmet. All of her life, she sweated easily. Firefights in tropical environments didn't help matters. "Sorry we took so long. Had to collect weapons and mop up."

"The PLA dumped a lot of shit here," Grezda said. The Bulgarian Special Forces sniper spoke with a heavy eastern European accent. Her fellow team members teased her as having a cute voice. Everyone else, on the other hand, thought she sounded like a Russian mob boss. She didn't take offense—the only people she ever dealt with outside her team and family were considered subhuman anyway. "Looks like Torrez was trying to uncover it."

"I doubt that crap was dumped, necessarily," Donovan said. "I think stockpiled is the better word. I think it was planted here to be used in case major conflict broke out in this region."

Donovan stood next to Grezda, towering over the rest of the team thanks to his six-foot-eight height. Kittner remembered when he first hired him. At first, he wasn't sure such a large guy would be able to successfully pull off stealthy operations. As it turned out, Donovan was able to disappear and reappear like a ghost. How the guy did it, Kittner would never know. But he was good at his job and was a crack shot with his sniper rifle, proving capable of hitting fast-moving targets at four hundred yards out.

"I agree with that," Metwally said in his gravelly voice. "There aren't just bombs being stored here. I saw some of the containers. Looks like some chemical weapons were buried on this island. Mustard gas type of shit. Not something they want the rest of the world to know they plan to use, until the shit hits the fan, that is."

"More importantly, somebody tipped them off that it was here," Kittner said. "We can find that out some other time. All I care about right now is finding Zahara."

"There are fifty islands in the Citadel Chain," Grezda said. "A lot of them are a few miles in diameter. Plenty large enough to house a secret lab. Zahara could be on any one of them."

“Would have been nice if our contact could have provided us with better intel,” Metwally growled.

“He can’t tell us what he doesn’t know,” Herschel said. “The guy only knew this group was operating in the Citadel Chain.”

Metwally rolled his eyes at that statement. His mouth was always bent in what the rest of the team called a smile-sneer, because it somehow managed to pass as both. It was a facial expression that started during a bad session at some casino in the Midwest a few years back. Starting roughly six months ago, it became prominent on his face.

“You alright there, Metwally?” Roach said. “Didn’t hear from you last week. Take another big loss? Considering the dough we make, it’d have to be a significant one to put yourself that far in the hole.”

Metwally tilted his head, the crooked expression definitely a sneer.

“Speaking of holes, how ‘bout I tear you a new *asshole*.”

“Alright, knock it off,” Kittner said.

At that moment, they turned to the sound of a chuckling Torrez. He sat himself up and greeted his captors with a toothy grin.

“Trouble getting along, I see. You Americans, I thought you have become too soft to be feisty.”

“We’re not all Americans, dumbass,” Grezda replied.

“You accept American dollars. You spend it. Maybe you do not wave the flag, but you are part of the system.”

“You talk pretty tough for a guy who just got his ass handed to him,” Alston said.

Torrez hit the man with a hard stare. “Undo these restraints and I’ll show you tough.”

Alston gladly took a step forward, only for Sorenson to grab him by the shoulder and pull him back.

“Hey, man!”

“Stay back,” Sorenson said. “Boss has plans for him. They don’t involve you being all gangster.”

“I’m not talking about that… you’re stepping on my foot, bro!”

Sorenson looked down. “Yeah? So what? Your boot looks like it’s seen ass.”

Kittner grabbed Torrez by the collar and pulled him away from the gathering. A knee to the chin flattened the terrorist on his back. He maintained his sinister smile until he felt the Master Chief's boot press against his throat.

"Where is Zahara?"

Torrez attempted to spit at him. "Go ahead and kill me, American. I won't tell you anything."

"You're really devoted to the cause, huh?" Kittner looked over his shoulder at Metwally and Roach. Both of them were ready to put their interrogation skills to the test. "You see these guys? The one on the left was able to make a former Spetsnaz operative cry like a woman giving birth. And the other one? He may have a bad attitude, but he spent fourteen hours making Abdul Kabar piss himself. You know who Abdul Kabar is right? Iranian Merchant of Death, as they call him. Yeah, we're the ones who did him in. Not before making him sing like a choirboy. So, go ahead and enjoy this moment. I hope you feel empowered, being so loyal to the cause and what not. Because it's gonna end in thirty seconds."

Torrez, for the most part, was able to maintain his grin. His eyes, however, gave away a hint of fear. He knew his captor was serious. It started with the mention of the Merchant of Death. The man was simply found dead in what should have been a stronghold in Afghanistan. All of the men accompanying him had been neutralized, with no sign of casualties to the invading force. Nobody knew who hit the arms dealer.

Until now.

"You lie."

Kittner sniggered and lifted his foot from his prisoner's neck. Now the fear was plain on Torrez's face.

"Last chance to talk and still be identified as a man."

Torrez grimaced, then spat again.

Kittner snapped his fingers at Metwally. The guy was a sadistic jerk with gambling issues, but such a type was often useful in moments like this.

Metwally unsheathed his knife and began pulling a few bamboo barbs from his vest pocket. Torrez resembled an inchworm as he tried to scoot away from the merc.

"Let's see what kind of pitch you can reach," Metwally said.

"Go to hell!"

Metwally knelt beside the prisoner, his smile-sneer tilted upward as he prepared to do his worst.

Chamberlain's voice came through the radio, halting him.

"Hey guys? Hate to interrupt, but we've got incoming from the northwest. Single vessel, with maybe four men aboard."

Kittner lifted a pair of binoculars to his eyes and aimed them in that direction. Sure enough, there was a thirty-foot shrimp boat speeding in their direction. The men on board were anything but fishermen, unless assault rifles recently became standard practice in catching shrimp.

"Everyone, take cover. Metwally, keep the prisoner quiet. Donovan, Grezda, Costa; you three think you can pick those bastards off from here?"

"Can't believe that's a serious question," Costa replied.

"Want me to take care of 'em?" Chamberlain asked.

"Negative. Keep the chopper hidden until we call you," Kittner answered. "We need to eliminate these guys quickly before they can alert Zahara. Otherwise, the bastard will dig in like a damn termite. I'd like to take him alive if possible."

"Alright. Laying low."

Kittner lowered his binoculars and gripped his H&K. "Snipers, get in position. Herschel, I want you, Roach, and Tajima to assemble over there by the—"

The distant sound of assault rifles made him turn towards the approaching vessel. Were the terrorists able to see the team from all the way over there? And, if so, were they seriously trying to gun them down from a thousand feet out?

He and many of his team members studied the situation through their binocs. The men aboard the boat were indeed shooting their rifles. Oddly enough, they were shooting *skyward.*

"The hell are they doing?" Costa said.

"Maybe they're pissed off at God," Grezda replied. She started to laugh at her dumb joke, then held her breath as the answer revealed itself.

What they saw was definitely not a sign from God.

The devil? Maybe. Because this thing looked like it came straight out of hell.

"What is *that*?!" Sorenson exclaimed.

Kittner lowered his glasses. He didn't need them anymore. The winged creature flying high in the sky was easily visible to the naked eye. Its head was crocodilian, its wings like those of a bat minus the fur, and its claws resembled Arabian scimitar blades.

It was at least forty feet from wingtip to wingtip and had a body length of roughly eighteen feet. Judging by its enormous teeth, and its interest in the people on the boat, it was definitely a flesh eater.

"Boss, am I seeing things?" Herschel asked.

"Yes, you are. If you mean 'imagining' things, then you'd be wrong," Kittner replied.

"Son of a bitch," Herschel muttered. "It's a damn flying dinosaur."

***

The past several minutes had been a nightmare. What should have been a simple checking-in had turned into a race through some horrible prehistoric landscape.

Jarran kept the boat moving at full throttle. His twelve-man team had been reduced to four. Six had gone down on Boat 2, claimed by that *thing* in the water. Less than a half-mile from the north dock, it had ambushed them. When Zahara's crew initially arrived on the island, it must have been somewhere else, for its presence was entirely unknown up until now. The only clue to its existence was in the files in the station's lab.

It raised its arms from the water like angry serpents and consumed the second vessel and all the souls aboard. The only positive in that scenario was that it allowed Jarran's team an opportunity to gain distance from the colossal beast.

A few minutes later, a new threat reared its ugly head. This one did not come from the sea, but from the sky. It had the teeth of a viperfish, wings of a gargoyle, and the ferocity like a demon.

In its first attack, it snatched Melhem from the deck and carried him high into the sky before tearing him in half with its jaws. On its return flight, it sliced the American Derek Yate down the middle with its talons. The man fell to his knees, the last of his energy spent trying to hold his guts inside. When the life left his body, the others threw him overboard in hopes of baiting the creature. It didn't work. It was as if the thing wasn't even hungry, but just hellbent on killing.

He couldn't turn back and risk facing the wrath of the thing in the sea. Like a pretorian guard, it went after anything that ventured near the shores. His only hope was to complete the journey to Sulfur Shores and hope his men could shoot the damn thing out of the sky.

Tomas and Jeramiah were at the transom, firing AK-47s at the flying fiend. Jarran saw the thing jerk to the left and let out a shriek. One of those bullets managed to hit the thing. Yet, it remained undeterred.

Dripping saliva between its teeth, it tucked its wings in and divebombed directly for the vessel.

Panic seized the team leader.

"Shoot it! SHOOT IT!"

Its wings expanded and the creature swooped over the deck.

SPLAT!

Jeramiah and Tomas' screams trailed off in the distance, their arms flailing as they were carried away. Their legs, on the other hand, quivered on the deck next to their dropped weapons.

Jarran stared in utter shock, watching the open pelvises of both men *standing* there, blood spouting from the top like a fountain in Satan's backyard. Those talons had literally cut the men in half.

The knees shook and gave out, spilling a few intestines and bladder contents onto the deck. His remaining comrade, Choi the North Korean, racked his pistol's slide. The weapon had jammed during the assault and he was having a hard time clearing it.

Two splashes marked the final burial ground for Tomas and Jeramiah, their torsos discarded by the creature in favor of the two living humans on the boat.

Choi snatched one of the blood-soaked AK-47s off the deck and squeezed the trigger. A moment later, the gun, and Choi's head, flew in a high arc over the console.

Jarran ducked down, seeing the beast passing over him, as well as the two splashes in the water. He turned around in time to witness Choi's headless body shivering in the middle of the deck, the hands still trying to grasp the assault rifle. As though a light switch was flicked off, the body shut down and collapsed next to the other remains.

Jarran was alone. The creature was circling back from the east. Its head was turned towards him, the eyes appearing taunting, as though it knew it sparked fear into the deepest depths of his soul.

"Get away from me!"

He picked up his own weapon and started firing. The flying reptilian twitched, absorbing some of the lead spray as it came at him.

Jarran turned his eyes to the shore. He still had a few hundred feet to go. The thing was fifty feet from his left shoulder and moving ten times the speed of his boat.

He shifted his weapon, placed the muzzle under his chin, and squeezed the trigger.

CLICK!

As it turned out, he had emptied his entire magazine at the creature, foiling his opportunity of a quick death.

The creature, changing its tactics, came down on top of Jarran. Talons literally pinned him to the deck, the terrorist gagging as the huge blades twisted inside his abdomen and belly.

The predator let out a triumphant screech, then leaned down to behead him with its jaws. Jarran could do nothing but squirm as he felt the two sides of its mouth slowly driving stake-like teeth into his skull.

CRUNCH!

The creature gorged on the head and shoulders of this latest victim. With no humans alive, it was no longer distracted by the urge to kill. It peeled the flesh from the corpse, tasting the warmth of the blood-soaked muscle tissue.

Like a bird, it bobbed its head. It sensed motion from nearby. The creature turned its eyes to the nearby shore. A split-second later, it had completely forgotten about its recent kill, for its focus was devoted entirely to the group of humans in black scattered on the beach.

Memories of its treatment in captivity strobed in its brain. Every instance of needles pricking its thick skin and electric rods jolting it into submission served as fuel for its hatred.

The creature flapped its wings and initiated its attack.

***

"Good Christ!" Kittner growled. He raised his H&K and fired a few bursts at the oncoming fiend. The creature glided like an Air Force drone, wings cleaving the sky in a straight, fluid motion.

His sniper team fired a few shots. The target, despite its immense size, proved hard to hit. It angled upward and circled high above the beach like a crow. After two passes, it swooped down for its first assault.

Kittner fired a few shots, only to realize the thing wasn't stopping, and made a run for the boat. The rest of the team scattered, with some of them going for the safety of the trees.

Donovan remained in place, seated on the sand, rifle pointed upward. The gun recoiled against his body, his shot landing right on the creature's left shoulder. It let out a shrill cry and veered to the right, its massive wingspan and velocity kicking up a cloud of sand as it passed over the beach.

The deterrence was brief, the fiend determined to resume its reign of terror.

Kittner watched from the aft deck of the boat, monitoring the thing's movements and speed.

"It's turning north, altitude forty feet, speed around eighty miles an hour. It'll circle back in about five seconds. Donovan, aim five degrees in front of it."

The sniper was now on his belly and panning his rifle, placing his crosshairs in the creature's path. He squeezed the trigger.

The bird shrieked and went into a spiral. It hit the water and disappeared under a massive splash.

Grezda whistled and stepped out from the cover of the tree line. "Nice work, Donovan. Couldn't have done much better myself."

"In other news, water is wet," Donovan replied.

The rest of the team emerged, each in awe of what they had just witnessed. Metwally slapped his hand against his thigh and shook his head.

"Can somebody tell me what the hell that thing was?"

The team stood in silence, looking to each other for answers. Finally, Alston spoke up.

"Fine, I'll say it. Looked like a damn *dinosaur* to me."

"Don't think so," Costa said.

Sorenson snorted. "Uh-huh, sure, okay. Thing only looked like a freaking, what's it called?"

"Pterodactyl?" Alston said.

"Yeah, that," Sorenson said, pointing a finger. "Don't know about you, but that didn't look like a normal bird."

"Pterodactyls have beaks," Grezda said.

"Actually, we might be thinking of Pteranodons," Alston added.

"What's the difference?" Sorenson asked.

"They're uh… um…" Alston shrugged.

"The proper phrase is they *had* beaks," Roach said. "They're extinct."

"Evidently not," Costa said, pointing at the water where the creature fell.

Donovan stood up, rifle at port arms. "They are now."

The team looked at each other, then sported a smile. After a few moments, they started breaking into laughter.

SPLASH!!!

All eyes turned back to the water. Like a demon ascending from hell, the flying reptilian extended its wings and took to the sky.

The laughter ceased.

Sorenson looked to Donovan. "You were saying?"

The beast lifted itself a hundred feet over the water, its gaze and toothy grin facing the mercenaries. There was no sign of significant injury. It was as though Donovan's sniper round was nothing more than a haymaker, momentarily knocking the creature down without inflicting any lasting damage.

Alston started backing toward the trees. "It looks pissed."

"You guys need assistance?"

Kittner raised his finger to his earpiece. "Chamberlain, you have the chopper ready?"

"On my way."

Having seen the thing from his hideout, the pilot was already prepared to render assistance. It was a quality Kittner appreciated in the Royal Air Force veteran, now more than ever. Who would ever guess he would need air support against a prehistoric monstrosity?

The creature faced the team and began its descent, talons outstretched and ready to dice them as it had done to the specters. It altered its angle, having detected movement in the air with it.

Like a massive dragonfly, the chopper rose from the north shore and sped into action. The creature flapped its wings, watching its mechanical adversary. There was a sense of confusion in the way it moved and chirped.

Probably hasn't seen a plane or helicopter before, Kittner thought. *It's going to be REALLY surprised by what happens next.*

"Hot damn!" Chamberlain exclaimed. *"Did NOT expect the day to take this weird turn."*

"Stop jaw'n and shoot the damn thing, would ya?" Kittner replied.

A set of machine guns rattled through the air, unleashing a violent stream of lead at the creature. The reptilian danced in midair, clouds of blood bursting from its body.

Squealing in agony, it reeled backward and hit the water. A splash of red and blue water rolled in all directions.

Wings continued slapping the ocean, the flyer lost in a frenzy of pain and confusion.

Chamberlain continued to punish the thing with an endless stream of machine gun fire. After a few moments, the flapping motion transformed into a spasm of wings and teeth.

The splashing ceased and the ocean gradually calmed, the epicenter of the waves clouded with blood and body parts.

Chamberlain hovered over the kill zone. *"That did the trick."*

"You sure?" Herschel asked.

"Oh, yeah. Very sure. The thing had tough skin, but now it looks like Swiss cheese."

The team breathed a collective sigh of relief.

"Nice work, Chamberlain," Kittner said. "Head back to where you were. Keep your ears open."

"Will do."

The chopper turned around and sped to its hiding place, leaving the mercenary team on the beach, still reeling from the bizarre occurrence.

"What's next?" Costa asked.

"The job's not done. We still have work to do," Metwally announced in a firm voice. He spoke as though he was the commander of the team, which came as no surprise to anyone. What did surprise them was his ability to focus back on the mission, as though they hadn't just been attacked by a winged, dinosaurian predator.

"So, we're not going to discuss what just happened?" Alston said.

"What's there to discuss?" Metwally replied. "Nothing's changed, except there might be a new player in the game. An aerial, biological threat. We already know the weapons on the chopper are enough to kill them, should any more arrive."

"But where'd it come from?" Herschel asked.

Kittner looked to the northwest. "Same place the specters did. There's another island a little over a mile that way. I'm willing to bet that's where Zahara is holed up. Assuming he's still alive."

"And… there just so happened to be a flying dinosaur hanging in the area?" Roach said.

Kittner exhaled. "I don't know the full details. All I was told was there were some kind of biological experiments taking place in the Citadel Island Chain. I think that explains the chemical weapons Torrez was digging up." He looked at their prisoner, who grimaced and stared into the distance. There was no point in interrogating him right now. He had Zahara's location. From the looks of it, it was more imperative than ever the bastard was stopped.

"You think that thing was an experiment?" Alston asked.

"I don't know. In case you haven't noticed, it's the first time I saw the damn thing too," Kittner said.

Metwally shrugged and rested his rifle over his shoulder. "Frankly, it's the only thing that makes a lick of sense. You're not gonna convince me that animals like that have somehow always existed out here all this time without ever being seen."

"I guess," Roach muttered.

"But why would they make a giant pterodactyl?" Sorenson asked.

"Pteranodon," Alston corrected him.

"Neither," Grezda added. "Those have pointed beaks. What we saw had a mouth full of teeth. Like a… oh, crap, what's it called? Dimetrodon?"

"No, those have the sails on their backs," Sorenson said.

"Spinosaurus!" Costa exclaimed.

"Did that thing look like a goddamned Spinosaurus to you?" Sorenson. "No, I was talking about the four-legged ones… doesn't matter! That's not what that thing was."

Even Tajima felt the need to get involved. "Technically, they are not dinosaurs. They are a separate branch of the reptile family tree."

"Oh, that's a bunch of crap!" Alston exclaimed. "Whoever came up with that technicality obviously never got laid."

Sorenson wrinkled his brow. How his cousin came to that conclusion, he would never know.

Grezda wasn't ready to let it go. "Dimetrodon… dimatrodon… no, that's no it. It's Di-something-odon. *Dimorphodon*!"

Kittner glared at the team. The only thing stranger than seeing a flying prehistoric creature in the flesh was watching a group of battle-hardened combat veterans in full tactical gear arguing about the names of dinosaurs.

Metwally made a dismissing wave. "Well, let's stop blabbering about it and finish the job, shall we?"

It came as no surprise to Kittner, or anybody, that Metwally was eager to get back to business. The team would not get paid until the bastard was stopped and the supplies recovered. But it was a fact that the situation had changed. As much as Kittner wanted Zahara captured, he wasn't willing to unnecessarily risk the lives of his men. The fact of the matter was there was a danger they were not privy to. For all they knew, there were other violent organisms waiting on that island.

"I'll leave it up to you guys," he said. "You want to proceed, or bug out?"

The team looked at each other.

"Oh, hell. We killed the damn thing," Metwally said. "You said so yourself. If another one shows up, we'll have Chamberlain blast it out of the sky too. Easy Peezy."

Kittner waited for the response from the others.

Grezda shrugged. “Last few missions have been pretty much copy and paste. This one’s already proven much more interesting.”

“Hell of a thing to add to the resume,” Roach said. “Shooting dinosaur birds, I mean.”

The rest of the team approached the docks, ready to commit to the task.

It was good enough for Kittner.

“I suspect one of two things,” he said. “Those guys were coming this way because they were fleeing the island, or because they were checking up on Torrez and were attacked on the ride over. Either way, Zahara doesn’t know we’re here. We need to let him think nothing’s wrong. With that in mind, I’d rather not approach with the chopper. If anyone’s near the shore, they’ll see it from a mile away.”

“So, we take the boat,” Metwally said.

Kittner nodded, then put his finger to his mic. “Chamberlain, remain on standby. Keep the engine running. We’re going for a cruise.”

“You got it, boss.”

Kittner grabbed Torrez by the shirt and led him and the others to the boat. “Hope you guys don’t get seasick.”

CHAPTER 5

"The hell happened here?!"

The terrorists surrounding Zahara looked to one another in hopes one of their numbers would have an explanation for the destruction of their outpost. A line of tropical tents, each capable of sheltering twelve people, were reduced to ribbons. The rations had been torn apart and spoiled. Same with the water supply.

Sadie felt her mouth dry up and her throat tighten. It was bad enough she and Lewy were taken prisoner by this band of cutthroats, but now they were even more on edge. In all likelihood, they would connect the destruction of their campsite with the simultaneous arrival of the two strangers.

She glanced at Lewy, who quickly mouthed, "Don't say anything."

It was advice she gladly took.

The men continued to rummage through the camp, a few of them trying their best to come up with an answer. During the ordeal, Sadie managed to catch a few of their names.

The one she assumed to be next in charge in this particular group was a stern-looking figure named Allard. He was South American; Sadie's guess was Columbia. When it came to interacting with the other terrorists and their hostages, he had a deep, harsh demeanor. When it came to interacting with a pissed off Zahara, he was suddenly an agreeable, pleasing figure.

Another one was an Asian named Kwangsun. Sadie pegged him from one of the Koreas. His involvement with the specter group was as odd as the clan itself. And just as evil. She wondered if he was from the north, which made sense in a way, as Zahara generally targeted areas associated with the West. It made a little bit of sense for a few nations to quietly send a few 'private citizens' to add to the manpower.

A third name she caught was Eman. He was of Egyptian ethnicity and evidently very proud of it, given the scimitar sword he carried, similar to those used by the ancient Medjai. Instead of serving as a desert ranger, he pledged his loyalty to the destructive and deceptive specters.

He, like Allard, was a tough looking individual—except when it came to Zahara. In this particular moment, they were especially nervous. Something strange was going on, and it was making their leader increasingly impatient.

Allard circled the burned-out campfire, where the men guarding this camp had been prepping some rations. Aside from the cooking utensils and camping grill, the only sign they were ever here were their discarded weapons. Allard checked one of the magazines, then looked at Zahara.

"Several shots were fired."

"Same with the other one," Eman added, holding the second rifle.

Zahara's fiery eyes turned toward Sadie and Lewy. She withheld the temptation to plead her innocence, but followed her friend's advice on keeping her mouth shut.

"Radio Jarran," Zahara said to Allard, still staring at Sadie. The Columbian stepped away and lifted his long-distance radio to his lips. He made three attempts to get in touch with Jarran, only to receive nothing but radio traffic.

"No response."

"Try Torrez," Zahara demanded.

Allard spent the next two minutes trying to communicate with the second-in-command, only to obtain the same result.

All the while, Sadie found herself studying the equipment littered around the campsite. In addition to the three tents, there were several large packs designed for hauling over a hundred pounds of supplies. One of them lay only a few yards away, close enough that she could see there was nothing in it. Given the number of packs versus the number of tents, it was clear they were not solely used to hauling survival gear, but something else.

Sadie nearly gasped. They were looking for the same thing she was. If terrorists were after it, then the situation was even worse than she originally anticipated. Perhaps the organization that abandoned this post had gotten farther along in the project than she thought.

But then, why would they disappear and leave everything behind?

"Oh boy," Lewy muttered.

Sadie snapped back into reality, seeing a very frustrated Zahara approaching her. Without an ounce of remorse or sympathy, he grabbed her by the neck and forced her backward until she was up against a tree.

"Use your words, fella," she croaked, eyes bulging.

"Who are you with?! Talk now."

"N-nobody," she coughed. "I'm... independent. Obviously... came... at a... bad time!"

Zahara smirked. "Very bad time. So bad, it's hard to believe there's no connection."

"I'm just... a..." Sadie sucked in whatever air she could get through his grip, "journalist. Was, at least. Starting... to consider... a... career change, now."

Zahara looked at his men, still pinning her to the tree. They stared back with the same, stern gaze. All at once, they broke into laughter.

Zahara released Sadie and backed away, letting her catch her breath while they enjoyed the moment. Nervous and relieved to be able to breathe again, she fretfully joined in with a small chuckle.

She was very much her father's child, resorting to humor during uncomfortable, or in this case, dangerous situations. He had spent a little time in jail during his early twenties, and that was his way of getting through altercations with other inmates. It was a habit that carried into his marriage and work life, and was forged into the personalities of his kids.

The natural urge to make a quip arose again when the laughter abruptly ended and the sneering faces returned.

Zahara unslung his rifle and aimed its muzzle at her stomach.

Sadie raised her hands and clenched her teeth. "Definitely thinking about a career change. Should've taken biology more seriously; could've gotten a job at the hospital back home. But no, I had to come out here and prove my conspiracy theories."

"Will you shut up?" Lewy hissed.

Zahara grinned. "So, you know what's on this island? Why we're here?"

She shrugged. "I have a hunch."

"And I'm supposed to believe it's just coincidence that you arrived right at the same time my people mysteriously start disappearing?"

She shrugged again. "What can I say? I'm a victim of circumstance."

He closed the distance until the muzzle of his rifle was pressed against her abdomen. Sadie swallowed and shut her eyes.

"You swear on your life?" Zahara said.

"I do—because it's true." *Very true! It figures I would arrive on this island around the same time as these bandits.* Zahara pulled the weapon back, then swung it in Lewy's direction. The shipwrecked captain bit his lip at the sight of the muzzle now pointed at his belly.

"You swear on *his* life?" Zahara continued.

There was no quip from Sadie this time. She could handle her own life being on the line, but someone else's? An innocent person, no less, who was in this situation because of her to begin with? It was too much.

The worst part was there was nothing to offer Zahara but the truth. And he didn't believe the truth. In a way, she didn't blame him. Given the mysterious issues plaguing his group, if she were in his shoes, she probably wouldn't buy into the idea that the timing of her arrival was solely coincidence either. But it was and there was no lie she could think of that would satisfy the madman.

Sadie dropped her hands and took a step toward him. "No, he's just a boat charter. Don't hurt—AGH!"

The man named Kwangsun swiftly moved in and took her by the arm. Like a royal guard protecting an emperor, he was anxious to protect his leader. He placed a pistol to her temple and guided her away from Zahara.

Zahara looked to Lewy. "So, that's all it is, huh? Bad timing?"

The captain grimaced, his hands trembling. "That's putting it mildly."

Zahara tilted his head to the left, curious at some ink on Lewy's left arm. He lifted the sleeve, revealing a tattoo design featuring a black background and a gold combat dagger with the motto "Foras Admonitio" across the blade.

"Australian Special Forces," he said.

Both Lewy and Sadie cringed.

During their voyage, they had casually chatted about his time in the military. He had served in Afghanistan, assisting the U.S. military in numerous engagements against Taliban and ISIS forces. He had given six years of his life to his country before devoting his services to various odd jobs. Eventually, he started his own charting business, which had its ups and downs. Currently, he was in the middle of a down, which made it easy for him to agree to Sadie's generous offer. Of course, had he known it would cost him his boat, and possibly his *life*, he would have had second thoughts.

Zahara yanked the sleeve down and squared up with the nervous captain. "Sherwood Green commando beret, to be exact. Precisely the type with a skillset that any intelligence agency would want to recruit. Just another bad coincidence, am I right?"

Sadie groaned. *Yes, actually.*

In any other circumstance, it would be almost comical. The only connective tissue between the specters and Sadie's objective was their goal. Both were here in search of the remnants of Project Bloom, though for drastically different intentions.

She cursed herself for not being more prepared. It stood to reason that other factions would be interested in the fruits of that abandoned project. Maybe she could have hired an armed escort. It would have cost her what was left of her dwindling savings, but at least she would be prepared.

Then again, it would not have mattered in the end. After all, nothing could have prepared her for that *thing* in the water. Evidently, Zahara's group managed to avoid it when they came ashore.

All of a sudden, it hit her. The man, Jarran, was supposed to take a couple of teams to the next island by boat. Now, they weren't responding to Zahara's radio calls.

Oh, crap! I think I know what happened... and these guys are gonna pin their disappearance on US!

Another thought came to mind: If there was one creature inhabiting this island, what else could there be?

She looked again at the devastated campsite. This was not the aftermath of a firefight. Some*thing* large and vicious came through here with brute force and razor-sharp instruments. Whatever it was, it was not human.

"Wait!" she called out. "I think there's an explanation as to what happened here."

All eyes turned to her.

"I'm listening," Zahara said.

"The experiments that were taking place on this island. I think it affected the wildlife here. If I'm right…"

"Let me guess," Zahara said. "You're going to tell me that Bigfoot is wandering around." His men chuckled at his joke.

"I'm serious," Sadie said. "In the water, we were attacked by a—"

"That's enough," Zahara interrupted. "You have three seconds to tell me who you're working for." He shouldered his rifle and sneered at Lewy. "Three…"

"I'm telling the truth!" Sadie said.

"Two…"

Lewy shuddered. This was not the way he expected to go out. Still, he did not whimper or beg. There was no point. All he had was his dignity, and he was going to preserve it.

"No!" Sadie cried. Kwangsun grabbed her by the back of the neck and moved his pistol to her jawline. "What else do you want from me? I'm telling the truth!"

Zahara glanced her way. "I guess we'll see." His eyes went back to Lewy. "One!"

Lewy tensed.

"AGH!"

In the blink of an eye, Kwangsun's cries traveled far into the island. His hand was no longer on Sadie's neck, the gun no longer pressed against her face. She looked in the direction of the now-distant screams.

He was no longer there.

Zahara's men fanned out. He pushed Lewy to his knees and stepped toward Sadie, weapon pointed at her.

"What happened?!"

"I..." She glanced at him and the trees, equally dumbfounded. "I don't know."

"AGH!!!!"

Everyone looked to the opposite side of the camp, catching a glimpse of the man behind Allard getting yanked into the forest by a large, grey figure. In its brief appearance, Sadie was only able to make out its basic shape. It was bipedal, had a large tail, and stood at nearly seven feet in height.

Her jaw dropped. Even in the midst of horrific tension, she was lost in the awe and wonder of what she had just witnessed.

"Was that a... dinosaur?"

Zahara grabbed her and pushed her near Lewy, then began barking orders to his men.

"Go after it!"

Allard and Eman glanced in opposite directions.

"Which one?" the latter asked.

Zahara stammered, something he rarely did. He looked in both directions in which his men were taken, trying to decide on a battle plan.

"Uh, *that* way!" He pointed to where the second animal ran off to.

The other men looked. In the distance, they could hear the man wailing in agony.

They were generally eager to obey their leader, but this time they stood stiff. For once in their lives, they had encountered something they feared more than Zahara's anger.

Rustling leaves and bending undergrowth turned their attention to the southeast. A third creature emerged from the maze of trees. A shrill howl echoed from the back of its throat, freezing the thunderstruck terrorists with heart-stopping fear.

It lowered its head, exhibiting the four-inch horn protruding from its long, bulky snout. Allard managed to move to the side. The man behind him was not so fast on his feet.

He squealed, then spat blood as the horn pierced his chest. The creature reared its head, flinging the man over its back. It pivoted to the right and parted its jaws. The next terrorist tried to raise his AK-47, only to have his shoulder crushed under five-thousand pounds of pressure per square inch. Its teeth deep in the man's trunk, the beast lifted him off the ground and shook left and right in a frenzy.

A feral carnivore, it spun in a circle, swinging the writhing victim in its mouth.

Sadie and Lewy stood up and backed away. Immediately, one of Zahara's men attempted to stop them.

A flash of motion caught their eye. The creature's tail was coming right at them. Lewy and Sadie dropped again to their knees.

The terrorist's jaw dropped. It ended up being the only part of his head that remained connected to his neck after the explosive impact.

Dripping blood from both its jaws and tail, the creature continued its frantic spin. The man in its jaws was now dead, his body breaking apart inside that huge mouth.

Zahara found a break in the chaos and began firing his rifle. The creature bounced, feeling the sting of lead projectiles striking its hide. Deterred by the pain, it fled westward, vanishing as quickly as it and its brethren had appeared.

Sadie uncovered her face, mouth hung open. "Holy…"

Zahara stepped behind her and Lewy and looked upon his team. Only Eman and Allard remained.

"What the hell was that?" he shouted.

"Monsters," Allard replied.

"Dinosaurs!" Eman said. "We saw it with our very eyes. They are real!" He looked at Sadie. "She knows! She's a journalist. She researches things."

Sadie scoffed. "I appreciate that you think I'm full of wisdom. I should tell you, a lot of journalists are dumb as shit…" She cleared her throat after seeing all three rifles point at her. "I, on the other hand, *am* smart. Somewhat."

"What were those things?" Zahara said.

Sadie took a breath, amazed at what she was about to say. "Your man's right. It was a dinosaur. Fortunately, if you're a kid growing up in America, you most likely end up with some sort of fascination with dinosaurs. Some of us nerds actually retain this information when we grow up…"

"Will you shut up and get to the point?" Zahara said.

Her hands went up. "Unless I'm mistaken, those were therapods called Ceratosaurus. They have the horn on their head, and appear to be of accurate size based on what I remember."

"There's three of them," Eman said. "Just one of them managed to kill three of our men. And we're next."

"Stop your fussing," Zahara barked. He goaded his hostages with his rifle. "Move. We're heading north."

"We're taking them with us?" Allard asked.

"They might be of use," Zahara said. "If those things show up again, we can use them as bait. While they're eating them, it'll give us a chance to get away. Unless you prefer we use you…"

Allard quickly fell in line. He sneered at the hostages and tilted his head north.

"Move it!"

Sadie walked beside Lewy, their eyes fixed on their surroundings, anxious about what waited outside their line of sight.

"Ceratosaurus," Sadie muttered to herself. "This story is way weirder than I thought it would be. Hopefully, I'll live to tell it."

CHAPTER 6

"Ah! Finally! I got a signal!"

Sorenson rolled his eyes after his cousin's fourth declaration of getting satellite connection to his smartphone. The prior three times, his screen locked up, forcing him to reboot the device. Being in the middle of the ocean, internet service was not easily accessible.

Elliot Kittner stood at the helm of the boat. His gaze frequently shifted between the destination and the sky, the latter being in search of any other flying surprises. The strange encounter with the winged creature taught him anything could happen on this mission.

During his rookie years in the military, he was taught to be ready for anything. Today, that phrase had a whole new meaning. Kittner took it to heart, but he never thought he would have to be prepared for large prehistoric creatures.

Fortunately, the only thing sharing this section of the ocean appeared to be the island of King's Chamber. Its southeast shore was a half-mile away. From afar, it had a rather charming appearance. The beaches were smooth, aside from some rocks on the easternmost side. The interior was filled with ferns and a variety of tall, thin trees with branches decorated with small, green leaves.

Donovan stood on the flying bridge with him, repeatedly sweeping the shoreline with his sniper scope. He identified some wooden docks, but found no other trace of Zahara's operation.

Metwally stood guarding Torrez. He kept a hand on the back of his collar and his other hand resting on the grip of his holstered pistol. The prisoner remained quiet, doing little more than glancing skyward in fear of becoming lunch for another flying dinosaur.

Kittner had no love for Torrez, but found himself feeling somewhat disgusted by Metwally's obvious urge to put a bullet in him. The mercenary was mad at the world. He had dug himself deeper and deeper into financial trouble, and as a result, turned into a bitter man who blamed everyone but himself. There was almost a glee in the way he dispatched targets. If the people they fought on their last few missions weren't the scum of the earth, Kittner would consider dropping the guy from the team.

It may have been a violent trade, but that did not mean Kittner relished in the death of others. He was very thorough in reconning his objectives before taking on a job. If he believed there to be too high a risk of collateral damage, he turned it down.

Nor did he willingly accept jobs in which he, as he once phrased it to Herschel, was the 'bad guy'. In one case, he was asked to transport a 'harmless' group of refugees across the Georgia and Russian border. As it turned out, those individuals were sleeper cells who were looking to bomb Russian assets and government facilities. In another instance, he was asked to rescue a crew of fishermen who were being detained in a South American facility. He initially accepted the job, but abandoned it after discovering the crew was actually attempting to smuggle one hundred-and-fifty pounds of cocaine to the United States.

Such jobs were beneath Kittner and his team. Metwally, however, expressed interest in them, mainly because the pay was significant. What he claimed would go into erasing his debts only ended up on the gambling table. As a result, the financial pit grew deeper.

"Ah-ha! I was right!" Grezda shouted. "It was a Dimorphodon!"

"No, it wasn't," Roach said. "Look here. The page says it had a wingspan of four-point-eight feet. And look! It says they had a mass of under five pounds. Don't know about you, but the one we saw definitely looked a lot bigger than that!"

"Not to mention it apparently had blades for wings," Tajima added. "I saw how it swept over the specters. Its wings cut right through them like a katana through a blade of grass."

Sorenson punctuated his teammate's observation with a "Wa-cha!" and a karate chop. Tajima's lack of amusement was plain on his face.

"It does *look* like the one we saw, though," Alston said. "The head and body shape all looked generally the same as what the fossil record indicates. Just much bigger."

Herschel chuckled and pointed his thumb at Alston. "Listen to this guy. Sounds like an amateur scientist."

"Amateur is being too generous," Costa said.

"For real, though," Alston continued. "What are the odds of finding an animal like this in the same place as some hidden weapons depot?"

"You giving credence to the theory it was part of some evil genetic experiment?" Roach asked.

All eyes turned to Torrez.

"Perhaps we should ask him," Grezda suggested.

Metwally was quick to pull the specter to his feet and push him against the gunwale. "What do you know?"

The terrorist spat in his face. Metwally responded in kind with a backhand across his chin. Torrez briefly grimaced, then cracked a smile in defiance.

Kittner tapped Donovan on the shoulder and nodded at the helm, instructing the sniper to take over while he joined the interrogation effort. He stepped beside Metwally and rested his elbow on the gunwale.

"I saw your face when that thing showed up," he said. "You were as surprised as we were. Also, the more I think about it, I get the impression the guys on that boat were not so much coming to check on you, but *running away* from that thing. With all of that in mind, I have to assume Zahara is the stupidest person on Earth for going to that island, *or* he wasn't aware of what was on it. I'm leaning towards the latter."

"What's your point?" Torrez asked, his upper body still leaning halfway over the side of the boat.

"Your client; what information did he give you? What did he disclose about this island chain?"

Torrez bared his teeth like a wild animal. It was the look of a man who was backed into a corner, but wanted to stay true to his convictions and not relinquish any information to the enemy.

"You were sent here to stop us," Torrez said. "If someone told you we were here, certainly they knew what we were after. You mean to tell me they did not tell you?"

Kittner shook his head. "Our job was strictly to take you bastards down."

"Something we excelled at, by the way," Metwally added.

Kittner gave the terrorist a moment to let that little zinger sink in. Water splashed under his head, wetting his hair with a mist. Torrez remained silent, aside from a few growls of humiliation and rage.

"What are you here for?" Kittner continued. "It's in your own best interest to let us know. Don't forget, we're your only protection against whatever's on that island."

Torrez retained his rebellious sneer. "We weren't hunting monsters, if that's what you're asking. All I know is that some Chinese weapons developer was working on something out here. We were sent out to retrieve it." He lifted his head to look Kittner in the eye. "If you were sent to stop us, that means whoever it is you're working for wants it for himself. He's probably got someone on standby right now, waiting for word from you so they can roll in and collect it. And if he wants it so badly, it stands to reason he plans to use it."

Kittner took note of a nauseated look on Roach's face. The mercenary was repeatedly glancing back at Sulfur Shores, his thoughts obviously on the hazardous materials discovered at the specters' dig site.

The Master Chief's own mind started piecing together the facts of their mission. His client, Sam Penyard, gave no specifics about the business competitor who supposedly hired Zahara's team. And the info provided regarding the history of the Citadel Island Chain was minimal.

The truth became clear. The CCP contractor was developing chemical weapons. Kittner could only speculate as to what kind of chemical weapons they were. Given the level of secrecy and the lengths other people were willing to go to obtain the product—

including hiring a terrorist unit—it stood to reason the weapon was potentially game-changing.

Kittner turned his eyes back to Torrez with intent to resume the interrogation. He found himself not staring at the terrorist, but at the water underneath his head. More specifically, the rigid object floating in that water.

It was brown in color, had jagged edges, and longitudinal ridges running down its length. Kittner followed the item with his gaze, then quickly took notice of another floating behind it. The second object had a similar color and texture, but an overall different shape.

"Uh, Chief?" Donovan said.

Kittner moved to the flying bridge and looked at the surrounding ocean. Everywhere he looked, there were pieces of floating debris. Each one had its own shape and material. Individually, they were nearly unidentifiable, but grouped together, they painted a clear picture of their original form.

"Holy shit," Roach said.

"Someone had a bad day," Alston mumbled.

Kittner could not disagree. It was difficult not to come to that conclusion when looking at the floating remains of a shipwreck.

'Wreck' was being generous. Savaged seemed like a better description. The jagged metal pieces he saw were pieces of hull. Looking out at the debris field, he spotted several more fragments, in addition to decking, outriggers, nets, buoys, and other components and equipment. It was a shrimp boat, much like the one that was attacked by the flying creature.

"I guess it's safe to say the bird had its way with a few more of Torrez's friends before it made our acquaintance," Metwally remarked.

Kittner reflected on the creature's method of attack. It acted like a large bat or an eagle, keen on swooping over its target. Even with those wings and claws, it would have taken it a fair amount of time to do this much damage to a boat that was well over twice its size.

He shook his head. "No. This was something else."

"Something else?" a nervous Costa said. "Like what?"

“Chief?!” Donovan’s alert came with a heightened intensity. Kittner followed his eyes twenty degrees off the vessel’s starboard bow.

Fifty feet out were a series of ripples.

In a few short moments, fifty feet became thirty.

Thirty to ten.

The approach concluded with a gargantuan splash. A tower of water rose twenty feet over the deck and crested over its occupants.

When Kittner and his teammates cleared their eyes, they beheld the sight of the tremendous forces behind that wave. There were eight of them, stretching over seventy feet in length, their leathery bodies lined with flexible cylinder-shaped objects. Suction cups.

At the base where those arms conjoined was a bulky mass. Resembling a giant red balloon in its basic shape, it was larger than the forty-foot vessel. Two enormous black eyes gazed up at the vessel and its occupants.

The day had grown weirder. Kittner and his team were being attacked by a giant octopus.

“What in the name of—” Sorenson lifted his rifle muzzle and swept left and right, unsure of which tentacle to target.

“Pardon the cliché, but holy shit! I did not sign up for this!” Alston exclaimed.

Kittner pulled Torrez from the gunwale right as another tentacle emerged on the vessel’s port side. It slithered up the hull and crested over the deck, its tip angling towards the team as though watching them.

He turned his eyes to the King’s Chamber. They were less than a quarter mile from the shore.

“Gun it, Donovan!” Kittner said.

The sniper put the boat in full throttle. It zipped out of the collection of tentacles. The leathery arms closed, interlapping with each other. Their efforts to crush the boat in their combined grasp failed at the last moment. \

A jet of water ejected from the creature’s syphon. Propelling through the water like a gigantic cruise missile, it quickly managed to put itself alongside the shrimp boat.

Tentacles sprang like rattlesnakes. Each one found something to grab ahold of. Donovan reeled backward, getting a splash of water and slime to the face as one of the limbs smacked down on the helm. It coiled around the console, crushing it like a tin can.

The mast and outriggers were next to get decimated, as were pieces of the gunwale and transom where the tentacles latched onto the vessel.

With a sound of crunching metal, the prop imploded. The vessel was dead in the water.

They were five hundred feet from shore. So close, yet they may as well have been on the other side of the Pacific.

Kittner knew of only one way out of this mess. He tilted his mic to his lips and switched his radio on.

"Chamberlain! Get your ass over here! We're on the southeast side of King's Chamber. We need pickup, ASAP! Have your guns ready."

"On my way, Chief. What's going on? Is it another one of those bird things?"

"No. Think more *Twenty Thousand Leagues Under the Sea.*"

"A squid?!"

"Close enough."

"I'm on my way. Just stay alive for the next two minutes."

Kittner had no better plans. He turned his attention to a large tentacle bending over the port bow. Its suction cups wriggled and stretched as though each one was its own entity. The limb coiled, its aim clearly focused on the former Master Chief.

He beat it to the punch with a three-round burst. The tentacle arched in the opposite direction, a stream of blue blood jetting from its tip. Kittner pivoted to the right and put another few bursts into another giant arm. The tentacle released its grasp on the flying bridge and lashed violently at the air, its nerves on fire from the stream of hot lead it absorbed.

The rest of the team joined the fight. Rifle fire cut into the tentacles. For the first few moments, the tactic appeared to be working. Many of the arms came off the vessel and retreated into the water.

After taking a few hits to the mantle, the octopus submerged its entire body. Ripples traveled far and wide as the ocean gradually calmed. The vessel slowly drifted, the eleven people on deck holding their breath in silence.

The ripples dissipated entirely. For the next few seconds, the only movement in sight was the breaking of the surf against the island's shoreline.

Sorenson and Alston cautiously glanced at the water, the former whispering, "Where'd it go?"

"Maybe we scared it away?" a hopeful Costa said. She took the moment to dab her sweaty forehead with a handkerchief.

THUMP!

The boat rumbled. A series of large ripples fanned out from all sides. Another impact touched the bottom of the vessel. Then another.

Next thing they knew, two tentacles extended from the water. They folded over the bow and pulled down. Like one end of a large seesaw, the stern lifted forty-five degrees into the air. All hands lost their footing and began tumbling toward the wheelhouse.

What they thought was going to be a reprieve turned out to be the calm before an even more violent storm. Vibrations of crunching metal traveled through the boat. Scattered throughout the prolonged sound were quick bursts, like gunshots, or rupturing metal.

"The hell's it doing?" Roach asked.

"It has a beak!" Tajima called out. "All cephalopods have big beaks. Like an eagle's! It's biting through the bottom."

The vessel shuddered violently. In the blink of an eye, the bow section became significantly narrower. Tentacles, like worms in loose, wet soil, writhed around their metallic victim.

"And it's crushing the boat," Tajima added.

"Oh, gee! Nothing gets by you, does it, Tajima?" Metwally said. He looked to the shore. "Don't have a choice. We gotta make a swim for it."

Sorenson scoffed. "Yeah. Brilliant idea. Get in the water with that thing."

"Maybe you've slept through the last few minutes, moron, but we're about to be in the water with it anyway!" Metwally replied.

"Wait!" Kittner said. "Don't go yet."

"Wait? Wait for what, Chief?" Metwally said. "We're going down. The boat's coming apart. If we're gonna make a swim for it, we may as well do it while the thing's distracted."

"You can swim if you want." Kittner got on his feet and pointed to the southeast. In the horizon was a little black dot. It rapidly grew larger and nearer, the droning of rotor blades penetrating the sounds of thrashing water. "Or you can wait twenty more seconds and improve your odds."

Sorenson was next to stand up. "I'll make that wait."

"Me too," Alston said. "So long as Chamberlain can get all of us out of here in time." A loud cracking sound rippled across the deck, making his point. A rush of water could be heard underneath their boots. The hull had been breached in multiple areas and was rapidly invading the lower compartments.

Even Kittner was feeling a little nervous. He cupped his hand over his mic and looked up at the chopper.

"Chamberlain? You see it?"

"Good God, Chief! Did we land on Jules Verne's Mysterious Island, or something? What's with all the freaking monsters everywhere?"

"Dunno, but can you shoot the damn thing before it pulls us under?" Kittner replied. "Aim under the boat as best you can. Your guns are the only thing that have any chance of hitting the bastard."

"I'll see what I can do."

The chopper moved to the boat's starboard side and descended until it was twenty feet over the water. Its pilot managed to tilt the aircraft so its nose and forward guns were facing the water. He positioned the weapons, inched a few yards closer, then made a few more adjustments.

In the blink of an eye, a stream comprised of two-hundred pieces of lead spat into the water. Traveling at a thirty-five-degree angle, they went right below the hull into the thing actively crushing it.

A cloud of blue water billowed on all sides of the vessel. The stern came down on the water like a judge's gavel as the vessel leveled out. Another impact struck the underside, sending it into a tailspin.

Kittner looked to the west, witnessing a large surge of water which marked the octopus' path as it retreated from Chamberlain's gunfire.

"Nice work. Now, get us out of here, would ya?"

Chamberlain was already on it. He positioned the chopper beside the deck, the underside grazing the water's surface. No longer did he need the radio to communicate with the team.

"Might wanna get in!"

Alston and Sorenson were first to assemble at the door. Sorenson slid it open, obnoxiously pushing his cousin aside to allow himself first dibs at boarding the Blackhawk.

"Can't risk your fat ass weighing the bird down before the rest of us get in," he joked.

"You're a real jackass, you know that?" Alston said.

Sorenson grinned and went to climb in, only to be pushed aside by an eager Costa and Grezda.

"Ladies first," the former proudly announced. They entered the Blackhawk, followed by the two cousins.

Kittner remained on deck, keeping an eye out for the threat while his team exited the boat. Metwally and Torrez were nearby, following the line of mercenaries to their salvation.

"Move it." Metwally pushed the prisoner forward. "Unless you wanna be a snack for that thing."

"It took a shitload of .50 caliber bullets," Roach said. "Probably dying from its wounds as we speak. Nothing can take that kind of punishment. Not even a monster octopus." He sparked a toothy grin of confidence and waved his hand in the direction the creature fled. "Yeah, it's probably laying at the bottom of the ocean, taking its last breaths as we speak. Or, however octopuses breathe. Point is, I think we're good from here on."

His grin flipped upside down, his teeth pressing together as he watched a new surge of water take form a hundred feet off the port bow.

Herschel saw it too. "You had to open your mouth, didn't ya?"

Like a giant boulder tumbling across a steep hill, the huge swell rampaged in the team's direction.

"Chamberlain, lift off!" Kittner shouted. He could see the pilot's bewildered expression through the cockpit window. "Go! Go! Go!"

Chamberlain took to the sky with only Grezda, Costa, Tajima, and the cousins on board.

The mass of water struck the boat with a deafening *BAM!*

All remaining teammates fell head over heels across the deck.

Kittner rolled backwards over his shoulder, enabling himself to spring right back on his feet. When he stood up, the tentacles were rising over the boat again. Several reached for the sky in a desperate effort to grab the chopper.

He fired several shots, the targets jolting as they absorbed his ammo. Unlike last time, they did not retreat into the water. Though it clearly felt pain from the projectiles, the creature no longer appeared concerned about long-term damage.

With that in mind, he noticed none of the arms were bleeding. Given the amount of lead put into them, it was odd there was no apparent sign of damage. Either he and his team did not inflict as much damage as he initially thought, or this octopus had some advanced healing abilities.

Chamberlain banked the helicopter thirty yards in front of the vessel and fired the autocannons. This time, the octopus did retreat, its jet propulsion putting the boat into another tailspin. The chopper continued blasting at the rolling mound of water until it vanished deep into the ocean.

A sound of "SHIT!" followed by running feet made Kittner turn around. Metwally was on his back, his hand placed on his jaw. Beyond him was Torrez, who had managed to take advantage of the chaos to cut through his restraints and escape.

Metwally stood up and pointed his rifle at the escaped prisoner, his shots striking nothing but air after the specter threw himself over the side. Torrez hit the murky blue water and swam for shore.

"Son of a bitch!" Metwally yelled. He went to the side of the boat and took aim. The clouds of blue blood worked in the specter's favor. He had gone under, using the murkiness to obscure his position.

"Lost visual on the contact," Chamberlain said.

"Don't worry about it. Get back here and pick up the rest of the team," Kittner said. He handed his rifle off to Metwally and began unzipping his vest.

"The hell you think you're doing?" Metwally asked.

"Going after him," Kittner said. "He's obviously gonna swim for the island. I need to catch him before he has a chance to reunite with Zahara."

He removed his vest and handed it off to Herschel, who glared at him dumbfoundedly.

"And you plan on doing this without gear?"

"I might be a good swimmer, but even I tend to get weighed down by all the shit we carry," Kittner said. He tapped his sidearm and combat knife. "I got enough to get me by."

"You're crazy, Chief," Herschel protested. "Let's regroup and go after him as a team."

"By then, he'll be long gone. And Zahara will be aware of our presence. Thus, eliminating our element of surprise," Kittner said.

"That's compromised already, Chief," Herschel said. "It'd be a miracle if they didn't hear all the damn shooting."

"Maybe, maybe not," Kittner said. "What I do know is if Zahara finds out *we* are here, he might try and make a fast escape. Maybe with whatever the Chinese were developing on this island." He moved to the foredeck. "Let Chamberlain know what I'm doing. Set down by the hill behind the east shore. Plenty of cover over there to hide the chopper."

Without wasting another second, Kittner jumped into the water. When he resurfaced, the Blackhawk was nearing the boat. Those on board tossed ropes down to the others.

He clawed at the ocean, rapidly pulling himself closer to the island.

Several yards ahead of him was a bipedal mass covered in brown clothing. Torrez had finally come up for air. He glanced back at the chopper, then quickened his pace after realizing one of the mercenaries was on his tail.

A former Navy SEAL, Kittner was ten times the swimmer the terrorist was. Already, he closed within a hundred feet of the terrorist.

Yeah, you better run.

CHAPTER 7

Zahara raised his fist. "Shh!"

Sadie felt Eman's hand squeeze over her shoulder, stopping her in place. To her right, Lewy was stopped by Allard in the same manner. Neither hostage dared to move a muscle or make a sound.

Their three captors listened intently.

"I hear it," Allard whispered.

"Fifty caliber machine guns," Eman said.

Sadie shut her eyes and listened. There it was, the rattling sound of military grade weapons. It was coming from the southeast, either from the shore, or maybe even beyond.

When she opened her eyes, she noticed Lewy's upper lip was stiff. He, more than anyone else, seemed unhappy to hear the gunfire. Sadie connected the dots and understood the source of his new wave of anxiety. Gunfire meant a new player had entered the game. Zahara already suspected them of being part of some larger strategy to intercept him. The arrival of new players would only strengthen that suspicion. Maybe even to the point of execution.

The leader of the specters turned around, his eyes a blazing fury. Lewy's unspoken suspicions were correct.

"How many people are with you?"

Lewy groaned and shrugged. "I could tell you for the hundredth time that we came here alone, but that would only make a hundred times you won't believe me. So, I'll just say something like 'I don't know'."

His sarcasm was rewarded with a blow to the back of the head by Allard. Lewy's knees hit the ground. Next was his face after his escort kicked him between the shoulder blades.

Allard looked at Sadie with a threatening sneer, conveying the possibility of her receiving the same treatment. Her natural defense mechanism kicked in. Humor.

"You know, I hear Sylvester Stallone was doing another *Expendables* movie. Maybe he's over there filming it. Hey! You guys could work on set as extras!"

Eman grabbed her hair. "How many people are with you?!"

Sadie disregarded the pain in her scalp and continued with her scheme. "Well, there's you, Allard, Zahara, and Lewy… so that makes four."

Eman pulled again. "Go ahead. Continue with the jokes, woman. See how well that works for you."

"Gosh, you sound like my mother!" she croaked. "She was a hair-grabber too! Except she actually made it hurt. I guess not having a sissy grip helped a tad, unlike someone I know."

She sensed the rising of Eman's other hand as he prepared to strike her.

"We don't have time for this," Zahara said. "We can't stay here. Not with those things out there. We need to continue to the shore. Once we're there, we'll figure out who we're dealing with and how many of them there are."

"What about them?" Allard asked, nudging Lewy with his boot. The yachtsman pushed himself back to his feet, looking more annoyed than in pain. He shot a brief glance at the gunman.

"You better shoot me. Or else, you'll wish you did."

Allard held the rifle muzzle at his middle, his own macho ego welling within him. No way could this guy in a ratty Hawaiian shirt take him in a fight.

"We take them with us," Zahara said. "Might need them as leverage. Let's go."

His two subordinates went straight to work pushing their prisoners forward.

"Let's go!" Eman demanded. "Move faster. One false move, and I'll blow your heads off!"

"Oh no." Allard joyfully prodded Lewy with his gun. "This one's mine."

Sadie proceeded to move towards the shore, equally intrigued by Lewy's rising temper as she was the sound of gunfire. The mellow yachtsman was slowly revealing his inner barbarian. Oddly enough, she found it scarier than the flesh-eating dinosaurs lurking on the island.

***

Elliot Kittner managed to close within a few meters of Torrez by the time the terrorist reached shore. The anxiety felt by the fleeing specter grew more apparent with each glance he took at his pursuer. He was certain he had a wide lead and was in the clear, only to be surprised when he discovered the former Navy SEAL could swim like a dolphin.

With no gun, Torrez was wise enough standing toe-to-toe with Kittner was a losing feat. The moment he cleared the water, he sprinted inland, leaving a trail of clumped footprints in his wake.

Kittner cursed at himself. Had he entered the water ten seconds earlier, he would have reached the bastard. Not only was the chase destined to go on a little farther, but it would now be under the cover of the island's natural canopy.

The moment his feet touched the bottom, they began pedaling him to shore. Five seconds later, he was on the sand, following the tracks left by his prisoner. Another five seconds passed, and he was surrounded by a variety of green vegetation.

Even on sturdier ground, Torrez had left a fairly easy trail to follow. After ten yards, he made a turn to the left, the bent grass and torn fern leaves betraying his intent to disappear. Kittner followed. The guy was desperate and did not bother being careful in his effort to escape. That was not to say Kittner believed recapturing his prisoner to be a cakewalk. A desperate enemy was often the most dangerous.

He unholstered his sidearm and made the left turn. There was no point in calling after Torrez and warning him to stop. Firstly, he did not want to give away his position to any other specters in the area. Secondly, it was a waste of time. Torrez intended to get away or die trying. The only reason he didn't call out to alert any of Zahara's men who may be nearby was because he knew it would give away his position, and Torrez was smart enough to know Kittner would get there first.

It became evident that the terrorist was slowing down. The pattern in his trail gradually changed the farther Kittner went. The steps were closer together, some low-hanging branches bent down, not from the impact of Torrez smacking into them, but leaning against them briefly to catch his breath. The swimming had probably taken up most of his energy, especially considering he wasted a significant amount of time hiding underneath the cloud of octopus blood.

Kittner saw it as both a blessing and a curse. For the one, it meant he was close to finding the son of a bitch. For the other, it meant Torrez was even more desperate, thus more dangerous.

The trail brought the Master Chief to a point where Torrez had come to a sudden stop. At first glance, he naturally assumed his target had stopped for another rest. Then he found himself puzzled, staring at the same oddity that had brought Torrez to a pause.

Directly in front of him were several thick ferns covered in dry blood. From somewhere beyond them, a fierce odor drifted in Kittner's direction. Having walked through more than his fair share of warzones, he knew the stench of dead flesh. It became so familiar, he could generally determine how long the source had been dead even before laying eyes on it.

Whatever or whomever was back there, it had been dead for at least a few days. Given the strength of the odor, there were at least four or five bodies. The blood itself was almost brown as tree bark at this point.

His eyes returned to the trail. Torrez had proceeded past the bloody ferns towards the direction of the smell. He was close. Kittner surmised that if the specter had more time, he would have changed course, but heard the Master Chief closing in and had to pick a direction.

Kittner cautiously moved past the curtain of plants and beheld ten yards of flattened undergrowth. Eight large lumps lay in the area, their soggy masses dripping with blood, slime, and other fluids resulting from days of decay and exposure. Bones protruded from each one, confirming they were organic. However, they were anything but human. Each one was roughly seven to eight feet in length, had smooth, silvery skin before death darkened it to grey, and had no limbs but rather a large fluke.

Dolphins. Eight of them, completely torn apart. Their bones had snapped as though someone had taken an enormous Viking axe to them. The flesh was torn outward from their bodies, exposing what remained of their insides, of which there was very little.

Dolphins? This far inland?

This could not be the work of the octopus. If it was capable of coming ashore, the surrounding jungle would be flattened by its sheer mass. The canopy above appeared completely intact as well, eliminating the possibility of this being the work of the flying reptile. No, this had to be something else; something capable of moving both on land and at sea.

Kittner forced the strangeness from his mind and concentrated on locating Torrez. Judging by the tracks, he weaved around the remains, then strangely took a sharp turn to the left at a gathering of boulders at the back of this bizarre graveyard.

At least, he assumed they were boulders. They were certainly large and solid, though their shape and texture appeared a little different than most rocks he had seen. They were almost disk-shaped, with little spines lining their surface. The ground around them was full of grooves and holes, as though a set of jackhammers had pummeled the area.

Two of those grooves were human footsteps. Torrez had made another sudden stop, much like he had done at the ferns. Strangely enough, he did not appear to go around the boulder things, but instead made a sharp turn to the left towards shore.

The ground where he had made the turn was kicked up, indicating he jumped backward before he changed direction.

Kittner approached the spot near the rocks and gazed in the direction Torrez went. His instinct was kicking in. A sixth sense, one that could be obtained through many years of experience, warned him that Torrez was nearby and had given up on retreating in favor of taking the Master Chief down in a surprise attack.

With his weapon gripped in both hands, Kittner studied the nearby jungle. His eyes searched for any signs of movement. Torrez was no amateur, but he was tired and anxious. Anyone in such a state was bound to make a mistake.

Creak!

Kittner's heart jumped. He detected movement, not from the jungle, but to his three o'clock. He turned to look. One of the three 'rocks' shifted. From underneath it came a segmented limb, like a spider leg. Uncoiling from its front came two bulky arms, each one segmented like the leg and armed with scissor-shaped appendages.

It began to stand up and turn to face him.

"Jeez—"

First a flying reptile, then a giant octopus, and now a big ass *crab*! Now it was evident what grabbed those dolphins and dragged them to shore. Apparently, Kittner had landed on Monster Island.

He backpedaled away from the giant grab. Shooting it would be useless. Just by looking at it, he knew his 44.-caliber rounds stood no chance against its shell. The thing rose in a sluggish manner, appearing almost annoyed about being awakened from its slumber.

He gained some distance from it. As far as Kittner could tell before he lost sight of the thing, it did not appear to pursue him.

"What the hell is this place?" he muttered under his breath.

Crack!

Kittner's brain lit up with warning signals, recognizing the all-too-familiar sound of a twig snapping. He pivoted and pointed his gun.

With a maniacal yell, Torrez materialized out of the wilderness. In his hands was a fragment of a large branch, held over his shoulder like a baseball bat. He swung the makeshift weapon, connecting its rotted end with Kittner's pistol. The weapon fell from the mercenary's grip, discharging a round as it spiraled towards some ferns.

Kittner stumbled back, hands empty, his mind instantly adjusting his strategy to accommodate the change in circumstance. Torrez pressed further, the club lifting back over his shoulder for another swing. Snarling like a wild animal, he made a wide swing. Kittner leaned back, the end of the branch coming within millimeters of his nose.

Torrez raised the branch high over his head. With a yell, he brought it down like a sledgehammer with all of his might, its end heading directly for the Master Chief's skull.

It was a highly telegraphed move Kittner easily anticipated. Rather than attempt to avoid the blow, he sprinted forward to meet the terrorist head-on. In the blink of an eye, he raised his hands to grab Torrez's forearms and simultaneously rotated his hips a hundred-and-eighty degrees. The terrorist's momentum worked against him, for he was flung over the mercenary's shoulder.

Torrez hit the ground and immediately started kicking. Letting go of the branch, he rolled to his right and pushed himself to his feet. He got himself upright, just in time for Kittner to close in and clock him in the jaw with a haymaker. The specter whipped to the side, shooting beads of blood, sweat, and slobber into the distance.

Frustrated, he retaliated with a swing of his own. Kittner parried the attack with a circular motion of his hands, then struck with a jab, snapping Torrez's head back.

Dazed and even more frustrated, Torrez tried again, only for the same thing to happen. Except this time, Kittner countered with a jab and a left cross. Torrez backed away, a steady river of blood leaking from his front teeth.

He regained his balance, only to lose it right away after receiving a kick to the chest by Kittner. Torrez reeled backward, rolling over his left shoulder and settling on his elbows and knees. There, he remained for a couple of brief moments while he caught his breath. Meanwhile, Kittner stood ready and waiting. The tactic of letting his enemy clumsily attack was working marvelously.

His eyes turned to the former SEAL, his bloody grin giving him the appearance of a man literally possessed by the devil.

"I'm gonna kill you."

Kittner snorted. *What's weirder? The existence of monster crabs, or the fact that this guy thinks he has a chance? Or his cliched way of trying to sound tough while getting his ass kicked?*

He shrugged. "Well, get to it then."

Torrez huffed and puffed, psyching himself up for his next bid to take Kittner down. The merc held his hands at chest level and waited. Torrez inched closer, fists clenched like a boxer. He wound up his hands in an effort to get Kittner to anticipate another swing, then ducked low and attempted a tackle.

Kittner was not fooled. He saw the trick coming from a mile away. As Torrez came within a yard, Kittner moved to a forty-five-degree angle, then pivoted right to put himself behind Torrez.

From Torrez's perspective, the mercenary had suddenly 'vanished' and reappeared behind him. All of a sudden, he was in a chokehold. Kittner put his foot on the back of his knees, wrecking any balance he had left, leaving him to 'hang' by the crushing hold around his neck.

Torrez clawed at Kittner's arms, each motion growing slower and weaker.

"F—fu—ck… you!"

"Shut up and go to sleep," Kittner said. He tightened his grip around Torrez's neck, feeling the last ounces of fight fade from the terrorist.

His victory was cut short by an all-too-familiar voice booming from the northwest. "Well, well, well! Look who it is!"

Kittner shifted, loosening his grip on Torrez just enough to keep him from passing out entirely. It was easier to use a conscious man as a human shield than an unconscious one. He whipped Torrez a few degrees to the right until they were facing the direction of Zahara's nasty voice.

After a few moments of silence, the evil specter emerged from the canopy. He held an AK-47 in his hands. A few fresh markings had joined the pattern of scars on his face, leading Kittner to believe he had his own share of misfortunes on this island.

Behind him emerged two other men, known simply as Eman and Allard. Kittner recognized both of them from his intelligence reports.

Two other people, dressed in civilian clothing, stood in front of the two gunmen. One was a man in a Hawaiian shirt, the other a woman with blond hair and in her early thirties. They kept their hands in plain sight, each of them all too aware of the rifle muzzles prodding against their backs.

Zahara kept his rifle trained on Kittner. "It's the second time you tried to take me down. How'd that work for you? I seem to recall the sound your friend made when I shot him in the face. Remember that? Even with his skull split open and a bullet in his brain, it still took him a minute to die." He mimicked a look of agony, then cracked a sardonic smile.

Kittner kept quiet. The remark was bait. Unfortunately, it was effective bait. What Zahara said was not hyperbole; it truly did take Jason Hall a minute or two to succumb to his injury. It was one of the most horrible deaths Kittner ever witnessed. The bullet in Jason's head ignited a series of spasms and put the pain center in his brain into overdrive. To sum it up, his last few moments were on a pain scale of twelve out of ten.

More than anything, Kittner wanted to snap Torrez's neck and make a beeline for Zahara. Unfortunately, the odds were not in his favor. The specters were armed and he was not. He would be lucky to make two steps before absorbing thirty rounds. Part of him was shocked that Zahara and his bandits did not ruthlessly sacrifice Torrez and open fire anyway. Loyalty only went so far with these people. Torrez was a valuable asset, but a replaceable one. Kittner, on the other hand, was a burr under Zahara's hide. If killing him also meant losing one of his top personnel, he would shrug it off and promote one of his other lackeys.

The fact Zahara allowed a standoff to persist indicated he was low on personnel.

"There's nowhere to run," Zahara continued. "Might as well let Torrez go. You're surrounded, American. I've got men all around you. You have no chance. Give up now, and maybe I'll let you live."

Kittner held his ground. Torrez regained enough strength to hold his own weight on his heels. His neck and jawline red, he bared his teeth in anger and humiliation.

"Best you listen to Zahara. You'd be a fool otherwise."

Kittner raised his knee between his prisoner's legs, smashing the contents in-between. Torrez moaned and unleased a slew of curses, unable to collapse to his knees due to the hold on him.

"Only a fool would think I would fall for any of your bullshit," Kittner replied. He redirected his gaze at Zahara. "That goes for you too."

Zahara petted the barrel of his rifle as though stroking a pet cat's fur. "I don't think you're in a position to question things. Whether you walk out of here on your own two feet depends on my next call. With a snap of my fingers, I can have my gunners open fire on you, then go about my day. Or, you can cooperate. Tell me how many people are with you, and where they are."

"Why? So you can plot an ambush for them?" Kittner said. "How dumb do you think I am?"

Zahara clicked his tongue. "I'm offering you a chance to live."

Another silent standoff persisted, during which the two hostages grew increasingly antsy. The woman in particular was shifting her glance between Zahara and Kittner, never once looking at the surrounding jungle. A vein bulged from her forehead. Her face turned red. Something was welling up within her; something she could not contain.

It all came out in seven loud words: "He's lying! There's nobody else out there!"

A blow to the back of her head put the woman on her hands and knees. Eman stood over her, repositioning his rifle after striking her with the butt. A frustrated Zahara shifted his stance and put his own rifle against the back of her head.

"I applaud your courage," he said to her. "Fact of the matter is courage will only get you killed when you're dealing with me." He looked at Kittner. "I'm going to count to three. If you don't surrender and tell me where your people are, I will blow this woman's head off. One."

Kittner said nothing. The woman was dead anyway, regardless of whether he complied with the monster of a human.

This place truly is Monster Island. And Zahara's the worst one of them all.

"I don't know," the woman quipped. "You sure you can actually land a shot? I saw the way you guys were shooting them guns earlier. Not sure you can hit the broad side of a barn."

Eman jabbed her with his gun muzzle to shut her up. The woman leaned forward on her palms, wincing while she overcame the overwhelming sense of fear. With enough willpower, she managed to shift her grimace back to a grin.

"You know? Back in high school, I was in gym glass with a girl named Sally." She looked back at Eman. "You remind me of her. Except, she hits a little harder. I guess Zahara filled his team with a crew of women with beards."

Eman sucked in a breath, his eyes going to Zahara in search of permission to beat her again. Even the terrorist leader appeared flustered at the remark.

Kittner had no idea who she was, but he liked her already. Too bad they did not meet during more favorable circumstances. Whoever she was, she wasn't dumb, nor selfish. She understood the kind of man Zahara was, and was not going to risk other people's lives in an effort to prolong her own.

"That's two," Zahara continued Eman's count. "What do you say, soldier? You willing to kill this woman?"

She scoffed again. "Do people really fall for that cliched drabble? Did you write a script and memorize it in case you were presented with a dramatic moment?"

"Sadie, will you stop?" the man in the Hawaiian shirt said. He spoke in an Australian accent.

The woman named Sadie looked over at him. "Are you for real, Lewy? Five minutes ago, I thought you were ready to fuck these guys up. What happened since then? Your balls drop off?"

Lewy's brow furrowed. Evidently, he was not used to such harsh words from Sadie.

"Hey, if you want to get yourself shot, that's your prerogative. Obviously, you're insane enough to come to this godforsaken place."

"*I'm* insane?" she clapped back. "Before we left, I asked you for all you knew about this island chain. Never once did you mention a giant octopus or dinosaurs!"

Kittner raised an eyebrow. *Dinosaurs? What?!*

He wondered if she was referring to the flying creature. It was the only thing that made sense from his perspective.

"I said this place was dangerous and many travelers were avoiding it," Lewy said. "One would have assumed that info would have sufficed. And how the hell would you have expected me to know a bunch of… whatever you call them… were running around. Certifiable-saurus, or something."

"Ceratosaurus," Sadie replied.

Kittner raised an eyebrow again. *Nope. Not referring to the flying thing.*

"Who cares?" Lewy exclaimed. "Like it matters how you say the name."

Zahara groaned. "Oh, for the love of God. Will you two shut up?"

His protest went unheard.

"Just evaluating the intelligence of the guy I hired," Sadie quipped.

“Oh, don’t talk to me about intelligence,” Lewy said. “You’re the one investigating the activities of some moron millionaire from the States. Didn’t you say something about a thousand tons of unearthed bedrock being shipped from Montana? Would’ve been nice to know that crap contained some dormant prehistoric monsters! Could’ve saved me an entire boat.”

“For godsake, that thing was full of rust anyway,” Sadie retorted. “Besides, I recall you saying something during the trip about your other business being more profitable anyway. What was it? You fly planes around; a small private charter. Sounds like a good gig. Consider yourself lucky. Also, if you insured your boat properly, it could be argued that I did you a big favor.”

“Ah! Yes!” Lewy gestured at the three madmen holding them hostage with assault rifles. “I’ve never felt luckier in my life. Also, I don’t think insurance covers sea monster attacks.”

It was a turn of events neither Kittner nor Zahara were expecting. The hostages were bickering like an old married couple, with hardly any mind to the fact they had guns pointed at their backs.

Sadie groaned and stood on her knees. She looked back at the terrorists, then directed a scolding jeer and a shrug over at Kittner.

“Okay. I’ve stalled them for an extra minute with my nonsense over here, Army Guy!” she said.

Kittner pointed at himself. “That was for *my* benefit?”

“Yeah! I thought maybe you’d use the distraction to come up with some sort of brilliant escape plan to get us out of this,” she said.

“Do I look like my name is Houdini?” he shot back.

Sadie’s jaw tightened. “No, you look like you’re standing there wasting time instead of improvising some kind of brilliant strategy.”

“Oh geez, Sadie,” Lewy said. “This isn’t like we’re in some movie. It’s not like he’s got some secret weapon hidden in the jungle.”

Crack!

The three terrorists and their two hostages perked up at the sound of movement behind them.

Lewy froze. His wide eyes were directed at the Master Chief, conveying fear, shock, as well as a hint of admiration.

"Wait…"

Kittner cracked a grin. In fact, he was using their delay to his advantage in hopes that the acquaintance he ran into a few minutes ago would track him down. It was a roll of the dice. Much to his relief, it panned out.

"Sorta like a movie," he said.

A wall of vegetation parted behind the specters. From the opening came the armored crustacean, scurrying towards the group on spidery legs. Its arms reached out and parted their razor-sharp pincers.

"A really *weird* movie!" Lewy exclaimed.

Eman and Allard spun on their heels and hollered as the big crustacean came at them.

Rifle fire struck the beast. They may as well have been throwing cotton balls at it. The crab kept coming, moving remarkably fast given the hefty mass its eight legs were carrying.

"Whoa!" Sadie exclaimed after laying eyes on the thing. She rose to her feet and backpedaled alongside Lewy.

Allard and Eman staggered backwards, the claws coming within a foot of the latter.

"Kill it!" Zahara shouted.

"I'm trying!" Eman yelled back.

With their captors' backs turned, Sadie and Lewy seized the moment. At once, they rammed their shoulders against Allard, who fell forward against Eman, knocking him straight into the clutches of those deadly pincers.

Like pliers on a piece of wire, those claws clamped shut over his left arm and the middle of his abdomen. Eman's jaws parted and conveyed his agony with a holler and a flapping tongue. The edges of both claws connected with one another, slicing through everything in-between. Blood spewed, bones splintered, and legs kicked.

The crab pulled apart, one claw separating his entire left arm from the rest of Eman, the other pulling out a shovel-full of guts.

Kittner took advantage of the newfound chaos. He swung Terrez around and knocked him to the ground alongside two of his teeth with an uppercut. He ran past the fallen terrorist at Zahara.

Killer crabs, giant octopuses, and prehistoric beasts were not enough to make him forget the objective. He had a score to settle, and he damn sure was going to see it through.

Zahara and Allard scampered backward to avoid ending up like their nearly dead companion. The leader, while unnerved at the sight of the crustacean, maintained his demonic resolve of terminating his troublesome hostages. He pointed his rifle at Lewy and Sadie.

Kittner cleared the distance in a few tremendous strides, concluding with a four-foot leap in which he thrust his right foot out. His boot connected with Zahara's temple, knocking him to the ground. The rifle shot wide, its bullet wasted on the jungle.

Allard spun around to see his boss on the ground and the mercenary standing over him. His allegiance to the cause overrode the fear he currently experienced. He raised his rifle at Kittner and placed his finger on the trigger.

Lewy charged in from his right and grabbed the rifle barrel. He shifted it skyward, putting Allard's shots into the canopy. An elbow connected with the terrorist's jaw, sending him stumbling to the side. Kittner moved in to join the fun, thrusting a kick square into Allard's chest.

The terrorist landed flat on his back, the rifle falling from his grip. He immediately looked to his right at the decimated remains of Eman and the crab picking at them. Gasping, he rolled to his hands and knees and scurried in the opposite direction…

…only to end up in the path of a second crab.

It emerged from the same direction as the first, its ferocity equal to its brethren. Driven by murderous instinct, it wasted no time setting itself upon the screaming man.

Its savagery was matched only by its strength. A simple snip from one of its pincers cut through Allard's thigh and femur. Spurting blood from the stump, the terrorist attempted to crawl away from the armored predator. Those claws seized him by the other leg, successfully pulling him closer before tearing that leg off as well.

Standing over the numbing specter, it began munching on the leg as though it were a chicken drumstick.

"Behind you!" Sadie yelled at Kittner.

After receiving her warning, he detected the sounds of running feet behind him. He spun around in time to intercept Terrez's attempt to tackle him from behind. A punch to the jaw put the terrorist second-in-command back on the ground.

"Behind you!" Sadie yelled at him again.

Groaning, Kittner looked over his shoulder. He expected to see Zahara coming at him. The truth turned out to be a third crab scurrying into the clearing, eager to get a taste of human flesh.

A couple of yards in front of it was Zahara, who scampered away from it like a scolded toddler escaping an angry parent.

"Let's go!" he shouted to the civilians. He pointed southeast. "That way!"

"What about you?" Sadie asked.

"I'll be right behind you." Kittner followed those words up with a kick to Zahara's face. He rolled onto his back, unconscious. The mercenary picked him off the ground and slung him over his shoulder before pivoting to retreat with the civies.

The crab was right on his tail, though only for a couple of yards, before discovering the easier meat on the ground. Terrez shrieked at the sight of those mandibles and eyestalks twitching above him.

Like the others, it wasted no time.

Claws tore into his trunk and pulled in different directions, raking flesh and rib bones. Heels bumped repeatedly against the dirt, his cries transforming into gargles of blood and spit.

Before long, the sight of the deadly crustaceans was obscured by an acre of undergrowth.

"There he is!" Sadie said. She and Lewy had stopped in wait for him. "Thank God. I thought those things got ahold of you."

"They will if we keep standing here," he said. "Come on. I know the way to the beach."

He tilted his head southeast and led the way.

CHAPTER 8

"So, what do we call you?" Sadie called out.

Her words were barely distinguishable through the battering of leaves and twigs as the trio raced shoreward.

"Kittner," he said, right as a bush branch slapped his face. With Zahara folded over his shoulder, he pushed through and found some open space.

"Nice to meet you, Kittner," Sadie replied. "I must say, you're like a wizard with your timing. I'd ask what brings you to this place, but it appears you're carrying the answer."

Kittner stopped for a moment to check their six. From what he could see, the crabs were not pursuing. More than likely, they were content with the easy meals that were Torrez, Eman, and Allard.

He looked down at his empty holster and felt a ping of regret for not grabbing his sidearm before departing with Zahara.

What he did have was his com unit. He activated it and raised a microphone to his mouth.

"Chamberlain? How's the team?"

"Wet, Chief. How about you?"

"Wet. But not alone."

"Caught Torrez, huh?"

"He's in the middle of a crab dinner. I'll explain later. I have Zahara though."

"Wait, you have Zahara?"

"Yep. Again, I'll explain later. We're heading towards the spot where I came ashore. We'll have a couple of passengers. Civilians. Again, I'll explain when I get there."

"Copy that, Chief. I've set down on the beach where you came ashore. The guys have secured the area and are awaiting your arrival. Herschel and Costa went out after you about a minute ago. I suppose they can head on back. Herschel, you copy?"

"I copy," Herschel said. *"Well done, Chief. We'll see you in a couple of minutes."*
"Keep your head on a swivel," Kittner said. "Zahara's men are all dead, but we're still not alone on this island."

"Oh, great. Let me guess: the local population consists of something along the same lines as our good friends the octopus and dimetrodon?"

Grezda's voice streamed through the receiver.

"DiMORPHodon."

"Seriously?" Herschel said.

Kittner smirked. "Crabs. Big ones."

"Crabs? Delightful," Herschel said.

"Anyone got a giant pot of boiling water?" Sorenson said. *"I know a good method for defeating those crabs."*

"No, you steam crabs," Alston said.

"No, you boil them," Sorenson argued. *"How do you not know this?"*

"You can do either one, shitheads!" Costa said.

"See you in five." He continued on with the civilians. "We're close. I can hear breakers up ahead."

"You ran into the octopus too, huh?" Sadie said.

"Makes for a real nice welcoming committee," Kittner replied. "I'm assuming it gave you guys a nice hello as well."

"We came from the northwest side of the island," Lewy said. "Either there's more than one, or the thing's constantly traveling around the island looking for food."

"Being gargantuan probably requires a major appetite," Kittner said. "So, what brings you two here? Looking for trouble?"

Sadie smirked. "I have a knack for finding it."

"I can attest to that," Lewy added. "I've only known her a few days and she's already cost me more than my ex-wife!"

"I'll buy you a new one."

"Yeah? With what money?"

Sadie laughed at that question. "Are you serious? After everything we've been through today? I'm gonna write a freaking book and make a million bucks!"

"Let's focus on getting out of here alive first," Kittner said. "Is that why you're here? Looking for a way to make money?"

"Not particularly," Sadie said. "I'm an independent journalist. I was coming here to investigate the connection between an American businessman with some Chinese experiments that were taking place on this island."

That got Kittner's attention. "An American businessman?"

"Yeah."

"There's thousands of them," Lewy muttered. "What's so significant about—"

"Sam Penyard?" Kittner asked.

Now it was Sadie perking up in surprise. "No. But that name is relevant to my story."

"Penyard's the business competitor of the man you're investigating?"

"Bingo," Sadie replied. "The guy I'm investigating is Damion Klavon. He's sold a bunch of land to a Chinese company. The land was out of Montana, where a lot of excavation was taking place."

"Excavation for what?" Kittner asked.

Sadie cleared her throat. "Fossils. At least, that was the official reason."

Lewy gave her an enquiring look. "How'd you know that?"

"Like I said before when the ceratosaurs attacked. I'm a dinosaur nerd." She gave a pragmatic grin and shrugged. "What can I say? I never outgrew them. Anyway, I was doing low-level journals on the world of fossils and theories, yadda-yadda, when I learned about what the company was doing. One thing led to another. I guess I was just bored with writing stuff nobody read. I tracked down somebody who left the company after a couple of unexplained disappearances; A paleobotanist named Dr. Ren Weathers. We arranged to have a meeting. He never showed."

"So, you got stood up," Lewy remarked.

Sadie's expression turned grim. "He was found dead, car wrapped around a tree later that same day."

Lewy turned away, feeling like a horse's ass. "Okay. I assume it's more than a coincidence that the paleo—uh, whatever you call it…"

"Paleobotanist," Sadie said.

"Yeah, that," Lewy continued. "What would be so significant about him? Wasn't able to identify the dino fossils, so the company offed him?"

"A paleobotanist is the study of prehistoric plants," Sadie replied. "I was not able to have a one-on-one with Dr. Weathers. What I do know is that he specialized in toxic plants and held theories of seeds surviving millions of years in dormancy."

"Jesus…"

Sadie and Lewy looked at Kittner.

"What is it?" she asked.

"The next island in the chain, southeast of here, we found a cache of chemical weapons," Kittner explained. He bounced on his heels, jittering the unconscious terrorist on his shoulder. "This guy here? He was supposedly retrieving a product for a competitor of my client."

"Competitor…" Sadie connected the dots. "You're a mercenary. You were hired by Sam Penyard. He was trying to stop Damion Klavon from acquiring whatever the Chinese were developing here." She held her hand in Kittner's direction. "Chemical weapons, apparently, as you discovered."

"What's Mr. Klavon specialize in?" Lewy asked.

"He's one of those guys who has his hands in everything," Sadie said. "Pharmaceuticals, oil, everyday home products…"

"Weapons contracting?" Kittner asked.

"I can't confirm that," Sadie said. "But I do know there's been accusations of him funding various research in foreign labs. One of those labs had an outbreak in 2015 and his organization conveniently had a vaccine for it by January that following year. Take from that what you will."

"Apparently they were developing something on this island," Kittner said.

"Yeah, but from what? You're telling me they found live dinosaurs in Montana? Even after everything I've seen, it doesn't add up. There's gotta be a missing link."

"Maybe." Kittner turned around and continued leading them southeast. "First thing's first, let's get the hell off this island and live to find your answers."

CHAPTER 9

"I'm gonna have to give the boss an earful," Herschel said to Costa. "Would've been nice if he had answered our radio calls."

"I think he switched it off when he was going after Terrez," she replied. She swept her rifle across the terrain. The beach was a little over a couple hundred yards ahead. Somewhere to their right, the Master Chief and his prisoner were moving parallel with them.

"Yeah-yeah, I know," Herschel remarked. "Doesn't mean I won't give him shit for having us trek all the way out here for nothing."

"Technically, he didn't *make* us trek—"

"You're really putting a kink in my rope, Costa."

She grinned. "You're just jealous you didn't manage to catch Zahara yourself."

He shrugged. "Probably a good thing I wasn't the one to catch that prick. I'd cost us a bunch of money, since we'd only get paid half-price if we don't bring him in alive."

"I can't say you're alone in that—"

Costa raised her firearm and pivoted to her nine o'clock. Herschel moved a few yards to her right and swept his rifle over the surrounding terrain. Both of them recognized the sounds of movement somewhere to the northeast.

They waited in silence.

The absence of sound only made them more nervous. Whatever had moved was large and fast.

"That was no monkey," Costa whispered.

"Nor a bird," Herschel replied. He panned his weapon right to left, seeing nothing but undergrowth and tall trees. "Let's move. On me."

Keeping his rifle aimed in the direction of the sound, he sidestepped towards the beach. Costa moved behind him, her weapon trained to their three o'clock. Maybe it was nothing. Maybe it was just some oversized cockatoo. After everything they'd seen on this island chain so far, they were not taking anything for granted.

Herschel turned his eyes southeast. The beach was just barely out of sight.

Just a few more yards, and I'll see that glorious ocean and...

Another motion to their nine o'clock brought them to a pause. Both mercenaries pivoted left and took aim. This time, they heard the eerie sound of running feet. *Big* feet.

"All units, we've got movement out here," he said on his radio. "Whatever it is, it's large and fast. We're being tracked."

"Copy that," Metwally said. *"What's your position?"*

"We're close," Herschel said. "A hundred yards or so from the beach. I'm not sure we can make a run for it though."

"Copy that. We're on our way," Metwally said.

Herschel looked at Costa. She was sweating a little more than usual. Fighting armed assailants was one thing. A familiar thing. An island of monsters was something else entirely.

"Cavalry's on the way," he said to her.

"Good."

Their hearts thumped at the sounds of walking feet. Whatever was out there, it was just out of sight. What was worse was the feeling that it *knew* it was out of sight, and deliberately monitoring their movements.

"Hold still," he whispered. Herschel dropped to one knee and kept his muzzle pointed northeast.

In that moment, he remained still as a statue.

A new sense of alertness came over him. It was not in the form of sound, but a strange tightening sensation around his ankle.

He had owned a pet corn snake as a teenager and remembered the feeling of constriction whenever it anchored on his wrist.

What he was feeling was similar to that, except several times stronger. And getting worse.

Now Herschel was the one sweating. His mind naturally went straight to snakes. God only knew what kind of snakes were on this island and how venomous they were.

Slowly, he looked under his shoulder down at his right leg.

Coiling around his ankle was something green, slender, and covered in thorns. Its surface was not scaly, but instead had a texture similar to that of large garden vines.

Its end worked its way over his calf. There were no eyes, mouth, nose—no head at all.

Costa saw it too.

"The fuck is that?"

Herschel went for his knife. The shift in his posture caused his foot to move a few inches.

In the span of a heartbeat, the vine tightened over his leg, securing a firm grip. He yelped as thorns punched through his pantleg and into his skin.

In that same moment, the vine slithered westward like a fishing line. Herschel yelped as he was dragged facedown into the jungle. He cursed with every breath, digging into the earth with his fingertips.

Costa's voice filled the radio.

"Something's got Herschel! It's taking him west of my position. I'm going after him!"

"We see you!" Metwally replied.

"I copy," Kittner replied. *"Have you identified the hostile?"*

The vine came to a stop.

Herschel rolled to his back and leaned up on his elbows.

There before his eyes was a spherical shape. Its base was anchored into the ground and surrounded by large green leaves which resembled the massive frills of a lizard. Vines shifted around the thing like squid tentacles.

But this was no squid.

As unbelievable as the sight was, there was no mistaking its identity. It was a plant of some sort, like a bulb of a dandelion that was yet to flower.

The tip of that bulb was ten feet high. The sides began to pulse, revealing the slits between its enormous petals.

With a wet, sticky sound, they peeled apart.

Four oval-shaped sides folded outward. Their inner sides were not like the gorgeous petals of a flower, but a slimy, thorn-covered interior surrounding a vile pit that went deep underground.

A horrid stench rose from the 'throat' of the plant like steam from a geyser. It was an odor Herschel was all too familiar with, only worse. The stench of decay.

Herschel had no idea what kind of plant this was, but he knew it was carnivorous. And he was the next meal.

"You've got to be kidding me!"

The vine began dragging him between two of those filthy petals. Herschel drew his knife and reached for his leg. He ran the blade over the vine, severing it. A translucent gooey sap spurted from the stub as the vine retracted into a pore on the inside of the bulb.

Herschel scurried backwards from the writhing mass. The petals lifted and fell like huge tongues, spraying spittle all around the bulb.

He unslung his rifle and stood up.

There was no time to move away. As soon as Herschel was upright, three more tentacles lashed at him. He felt pressure around his midsection, his left leg, and his right arm. All at once, the vines began pulling him in.

Herschel tried to fight, but was easily outmuscled. Grunting in fear and frustration, he fell to the ground.

"Shit!" He felt himself sliding closer to the nearest petals. "SHIT!"

"Whoa!"

It was Metwally, his exclamation repeated by the other team members as they assembled near the plant.

"We've got freaking *Little Shop of Horrors* over here!" Roach said.

Alston and Sorenson grabbed Herschel by the arms and used their knives to free him of the vines.

Roach and Metwally closed in on the bulb and opened fire. Watery fluid and chunks of soft, fibrous tissue erupted from the petals and pit.

Costa, Grezda, and Donovan joined in. Their combined gunfire acted as a giant invisible weedwhacker on the thing, shredding the soft petals and reducing the bulb to a soggy mess.

Herschel backed away from the thing. "Okay, this island can go to hell."

"I think this island *is* hell," Costa replied.

"All units report," Kittner said.

"We've got Herschel, boss," Donovan said. "He's okay."

"It wasn't an issue that could've been solved with butter," Alston added.

Sorenson jumped at the opportunity to chime in. "Dressing, maybe."

"What the hell is this thing?" Grezda said.

"I figured you'd know," Alston said. "You've proven to be the expert on prehistoric monsters."

"These are questions best left for another time. Everyone, get back to the chopper. Chamberlain, have the bird ready for liftoff."

"You got it, boss," the pilot replied.

***

Chamberlain sat in the cockpit of the Sikorsky UH-60 Blackhawk. The main and tail rotors rotated, kicking up sand and dirt. The fuselage door was open for the team members. Once they were inside the aircraft, all he would have to do was ascend.

He had been paying attention to the radio transmissions. If anything was for certain, it was that this mission proved to be weirder than any operation he had been a part of. And he had more than his fair share of odd moments.

Serving in the British Army in Afghanistan, he flew a gunship in support of SAS troops. Their target was a Taliban strategist and arms dealer, who supposedly was running a heroin operation in the area. The thing was, nobody knew of that little tidbit at the time.

When arriving at the three-story building where their target was located, he encountered armed resistance. Chamberlain took out the terrorist gunmen with a barrage of minigun fire. In doing so, he struck the foundation of the structure.

As it turned out, the building's foundation, which was poorly constructed to begin with, was heavily rotted. The hits from the Blackhawk's guns proved to be the final nail in the coffin. The entire building had collapsed onto itself, revealing a large sublevel where the terrorist's drug side-hustle was taking place.

That was nothing compared to other oddities he experienced.

Chamberlain had seen bio labs where strange experiments were unsuccessfully conducted on animals and humans. He had even taken part in a government operation, providing a military escort with blacked-out windows to a destination where the remains of some kind of craft comprised of an unidentified metal was discovered. Whatever its origins was, he did not know. All he could do was speculate—and his mind could only come to one conclusion.

It was an event he kept close to the chest, not even disclosing it to his teammates. Some secrets carried deadly consequences.

Much like whatever was going on here.

He kept his eyes on the tree line. The team would arrive any second now.

A swaying of some tall grass made him perk up. He twisted in his seat to look at his eight o'clock, expecting to see the guys racing across the beach to the bird.

A pair of orange eyes with black pupils stared back at him. In-between them was a long angular snout with tough leathery skin colored in red and black, with a twelve-inch horn at the nose. Serrated teeth protruded from the edges of its jawline, dripping saliva.

The head rose, revealing the long neck and the two small, yet deadly arms tucked underneath. The lips peeled back into a snarl.

"Jesus…"

He was looking at a dinosaur.

A hungry one.

He leaned over to unholster his pistol.

The beast charged at him with a terrible howl. Chamberlain yanked his pistol free and pointed it to the window, only to redirect it to the windscreen as the creature hooked to the front of the aircraft.

Driven by millions of years of aggressive instinct, it wasted no time going for the kill. Tucking its head down to a forty-five-degree angle, it threw itself against the helicopter.

The huge head plowed through the glass. Shards, like a storm of shurikens, flew into the cockpit, slicing fabric and flesh. The injuries sustained to the pilot went unnoticed, for a deadlier torment immediately followed.

Those huge jaws clamped down over Chamberlain's right shoulder, driving serrated teeth into his shoulder blade and pectoral muscles. A ravaging motion of twists ensued, crushing bones and eviscerating flesh.

Pain and panic did their worst on the pilot, erasing any shred of tactical instinct. He reared back, his hand clutching the joystick. A shift of the control took the chopper off the beach high into the sky.

His attacker dug its hind feet into the nose of the aircraft. Wedged into the cockpit, it tore further into Chamberlain, successfully detaching his entire arm from his body before going for his head.

Teeth punched through his eye sockets. The loss of eyesight was barely noticed by the pilot, as the implosion of his skull came immediately after.

***

As Kittner, Sadie, and Lewy neared the beach, they could hear the screaming rotors high in the air.

"What the hell's he doing?"

They arrived in the clearing and turned their eyes to the sky. The chopper had ascended two hundred feet high.

To their left, the rest of the team members arrived.

"Where's he going?" Alston said.

Grezda pointed. "What's that?"

The chopper turned, bringing to view the long and narrow object swaying from the cockpit. It was over ten feet in length, red and black in color, and connected to a larger body. Whatever it was, it had jammed itself into the cockpit to get at Chamberlain.

The helicopter pitched, then tilted to port.

Kittner, knowing what was coming next, guided the civilians back.

"Move! Move! Get of the way!"

The rest of the team followed with haste.

Fifty yards behind them, the chopper smashed down. Its armaments and fuel tank erupted on impact, consuming the machine and its two occupants in a ball of flame and debris.

A tremor shook the shoreline. Sand and water lifted high, forming its own storm of mist and grains. A gust of displaced air swept in all directions, momentarily blinding the team with clouds of sand and dirt. The thunderous echo traveled far into the sky, resembling the roar of a far-off thunderstorm.

Kittner took a knee, letting Zahara fall off his shoulder. The terrorist leader, having awakened right before the crash, faceplanted against the sand. Kittner put a knee on his back to prevent him from attempting to escape.

Next to him was Sadie and Lewy, the latter forcing the other to put her head down as the air blast passed over them.

The turbulent aftermath proceeded for several more seconds, after which the flames shrank and the wind calmed into a light breeze.

Kittner lifted his head and looked at the crash. The basic shape of the helicopter was somewhat recognizable. Its fuselage and cockpit looked as though a giant can opener had been taken to them. There was little trace of the pilot and dinosaurian attacker; just smoldering pieces of flesh raining down with the metal fragments.

Alston stood up. “That’s lovely. There goes our ride.”

His cousin forcibly grabbed him by the shoulder. The facetious vibe between them was gone. In Sorenson’s eyes was a scalding look.

“Hey! Chamberlain was in there, jackass! He’s *dead!*”

Alston pushed his hand away. “You think I’m not aware of that? I am! I’m also aware of the fact that we’re next!”

Herschel moved between them. “Cut it out, you two.”

Metwally made a deriding chuckle. “Why? He’s not wrong.”

“We can call a new ride,” Kittner said. “You know this, Metwally. As a matter of fact, you have the SAT phone. How ‘bout you get ahold of Echo-Charlie and get a plane or a boat over here.”

“Gladly,” Metwally said. “I just hope we’ll survive the fourteen hours it’ll take for them to get here. And that’s the best-case scenario.”

Costa put a hand up while shaking her head. “Hold up! Are we not going to talk about what we just saw? What was that thing?”

Kittner looked at Sadie. She was seated on the ground, reeling from what she just experienced.

"A Ceratosaurus, right?"

She nodded. "Yes. Same size, same coloring."

"It's dead now," Tajima remarked.

"Yes, but we encountered more than one," Sadie replied. "There's at least one more out there."

"That, and who knows what else," Roach added.

"Guys?" Donovan called in a nervous voice.

"I say we set a trap for them here," Tajima said. He held up a grenade launcher taken from the chopper. Roach had one as well. He sported it like a hunting rifle in obvious agreement with Tajima's idea.

"We could draw them out and give them a surprise," he said.

"Guys?!" Donovan said louder.

The rare anxiety in his voice, coupled with the pointing of his rifle out to sea, got the attention of his teammates. Everyone looked far out into the water.

Like a group of sea serpents, the tentacles of the giant octopus looped above the waves. They were less than fifty feet out, the huge mantle barely concealed by the surf. In spite of the damage it had taken from Chamberlain, it was active and clearly aware of their presence.

"To hell with this," Metwally growled. He raised his gun to fire at the creature. Kittner grabbed his muzzle and forced it downward.

"Wait."

They stood silently, watching the enormous cephalopod. After a few moments, the arms submerged. Rolling waves formed in the wake of the creature's motion. Its body was barely visible as a silhouette gliding under the surface.

Alston exhaled sharply. "I hate this place."

Tajima kept his grenade launcher pointed at the water. "Maybe I spoke a little too soon about staying here."

"What's your call, Chief?" Herschel asked. "You want us to set up defensive position here while we wait for rescue, or find a new place to set up camp?"

Kittner looked at the surf rolling onto the shore. He hated predicaments like this where he had to choose the better of two crummy options. While this place allowed for significant field of vision, it was a death trap. If that octopus came to shore, they'd be dead meat. Additionally, there was the threat of the crabs. They, for sure, would return to the beach at some point in search of more food. And for all he knew, there were several others waiting to come on land. Then there was the threat of other flying creatures. Again, a spot like this was a death trap.

On the contrary, he hated the idea of wandering through the island in hopes of finding a better defensive position. At the very least, he needed a concrete destination first.

"We can't stay here. We'll have to move."

"With those things out there?" Metwally said.

"No, he's right," Lewy said. He pointed to some abrasions in the sand. "You see these? These were made by the crabs." The team stared dumbfoundedly at him. All of a sudden, he realized why they were so confused. "Oh! Right. You didn't see those yet."

"The point is, we have more than the giant octopus to worry about if we stay here," Sadie added.

"Dinosaurs, killer plants, octopuses, flying pterosaurs, and now CRABS?!" Alston exclaimed.

"Flying Dimorphodon," Grezda corrected him.

Alston groaned. "Even now, you've got a stick up your ass for accuracy."

"Whatever the case, the boss is right," Grezda said. "You guys ever see video of octopuses coming on land? It's freaky! And a lot of them are surprisingly spry. Considering the hot temper that big one has, I'd bet money it's waiting for the right moment to come at us. Bottom line: we're doomed if we stay here."

"Serves all of you right," Zahara called out.

The short-tempered Metwally was quick to strut to the fallen terrorist with intent to exercise his fists. Kittner and Herschel stood in his way, both ready to physically restrain the debt-ridden mercenary if necessary. Metwally rolled his jaw, then spat. Conceding defeat, he walked away.

Kittner lifted Zahara to his feet and pushed him into Herschel's grasp. Standing face-to-face with his captive, the former Master Chief gestured at the burning wreckage.

"Your people are all dead. Like it or not, we're your only shot at getting off this rock. We can get a transport, but we need a place to hold up. Since you've been here a little longer than we have, I suspect you already know a place."

Zahara bared a rotten-toothed smile. "What makes you think I'm gonna help you? Maybe I'm fine with dying here, so long as I get to see you die as well."

Kittner nodded in Metwally's direction. "In that case, I might as well set him on you. Believe me, if it comes down to it, we'll make sure you die first. And knowing Metwally's temper, it'll be slow and painful. And for once, I won't do a damn thing to stop him."

Zahara looked over at the bearded, slightly out of shape mercenary. "Got a temper, huh? Something tells me you've got issues. And I'm not talking about the current predicament."

Metwally unsheathed a knife. "Nothing compared to what you're about to go through. I'm gonna start with the feet, then the groin, and slowly reveal everything in the meat sack above it."

Kittner grabbed the terrorist by the chin and forced his face in his direction. "Last chance. Where was your camp? Is there a facility on this island?"

Zahara took another glance at the hillbilly mercenary, then at the water. Kittner read the look in his eyes.

Cooperate now, live to fight another day.

The terrorist pointed his nose at the jungle. "I know the way."

Metwally pointed his knife. "No tricks."

Zahara smiled at him, then looked at Kittner. "No tricks."

Kittner, after letting Herschel bind the prisoner's hands, pushed him forward.

"Lead the way."

CHAPTER 10

The island facility was a paradox built from aluminum, steel, and drywall. A combination of high-tech state-of-the-art technology and lower-class living conditions, it was set up on moderately even ground, consisting of roughly three acres of land.

Several mobile homes were laid out on the southwest side. Kittner counted seven. An inspection of the nearest one revealed they were being used as sleep quarters for the original staff who worked here. A few meters beyond them was a larger support building adjacent to a garage where the maintenance crews and other support staff worked and ate.

On the northern side of the site was where the majority of the budget was used. As opposed to the comparatively cheap structures that made up the garage and quarters, the big building was made of high-quality steel and had a roof covered in all sorts of communication gadgets. It was three stories high, with no expense spared for the personnel who worked there. There were air conditioning units stationed on the south and east sides, as well as an awning extending over each exit.

Three large steel containers were placed on the west side of the facility. They were thirty feet in length, ten feet wide, and solid black with no windows. A small metal umbilical connected it to each one, allowing for access. All three of them had a ventilation system and were connected to an air conditioning unit, indicating whatever had been in there was living.

On the other side of the big building was the birdhouse. It was essentially a giant cage, standing forty feet high and twice as wide, containing several artificial branches and 'bird houses' for the occupants to settle inside. Judging by those houses… and the size of the cage overall… the 'birds' were large enough to carry off full-grown steer.

Much like a certain Dimorphodon they encountered earlier.

If these findings were not weird enough, there was the large dome structure north of the big building. Like an upside-down bowl comprised of thick steel, it was ventilated like the containers and attached to the compound via an umbilical. On its east side were a set of double doors designed for the passage of something incredibly large. The presence of a semi-truck and a forty-foot flat trailer gave further credence to the mental image.

Upon first sight of the campus, the team knew enemy personnel was not a concern here. It was a ghost town, rancid with the smell of dead bodies and burned metal and fuel. The mobile homes were wrecked, some of them filled with mutilated bodies. One was caved in as though rammed by a bus. Another was the opposite, with its front wall pulled outward. Those who barricaded themselves in both of them met the same fate.

The destruction was not limited to the sleep quarters. Every structure on this research site was damaged in some way. Additionally, multiple vehicles had been completely wrecked, the ground near them marked with zagging tread lines, indicating they were racing at full-speed when overturned. Those attempting to use them for escape were left in similar condition—completely dismantled. Other trucks were parked in the lot, where they were brutally smashed.

The south side of the support building was completely collapsed, exposing what appeared to be a freezer room. An inspection of the small structure revealed a kitchen and mess hall, all filled with decaying remains.

Bent bars on the upper right side of the bird cage showed where the Dimorphodon escaped. Directly below it was a heavy indentation in the bars, indicating something large had struck the cage.

That was hardly as alarming as the damage to the containers and the dome, particularly the latter. A huge section had been broken off on the southwest side, spewing thick steel fragments across the lawn. A series of gigantic footsteps had torn up the ground between the dome and the compound. Like a runaway train, it plowed through the three umbilicals, damaging the air-tight doors on the containers. Their occupants took advantage of the chaos and broke free, their rampage illustrated by the blood, body parts, and property damage.

"Geez," Sadie whispered.

Kittner stood near the garage doors, sweeping his rifle muzzle over the dried blood smears and discarded remains. Several tools had been yanked off the walls to be used as weapons, to no avail. The flooring was heavily dented as though an enormous jackhammer had been used on the place… a jackhammer with a three-toed chisel.

Herschel, Roach, Tajima, and the cousins stepped outside after completing a sweep of the support building. Herschel made eye contact with Kittner and gave a solemn nod.

"Just as bad in there as you'd expect."

"Indeed," Kittner said. He was looking at some supplies left from Zahara's specter group. "Though, I guess the people here were successful enough, given the fact someone was desperate enough to send this shithead and his goons out to get it."

Zahara, standing in front of Metwally's gun muzzle, spat on the ground.

"Don't act like you're so innocent. You were sent here to stop me, all so somebody else could get their hands on what was being developed here."

"And what was being developed?" Lewy asked.

"Chemical weapons," Kittner replied, his eyes locked on the terrorist piece of filth. "They stored the samples on the next island over. Zahara was sent here to get the computer files. Weren't you?"

Zahara did not need to answer. Kittner knew he was right. There was only one gap in the logic, and that was Zahara's clear lack of awareness regarding the dinosaurs. The men who hired him did not inform him of the presence of violent prehistoric animals. As far as he knew, Zahara was just sent here to retrieve chemical samples.

On that note, neither was Kittner made aware. Sam Penyard must have known what was going on here, and if he wanted the mission to succeed, it would not have made sense for him to keep the information secret.

Either both teams were set up to fail, or there was something more to the story.

"Why are you here?" he said.

Zahara's brow wrinkled. "You're asking *now*? Haven't you already figured that out?"

"Most of your people were on the other island where they buried the chemicals," Kittner said. "You took a small force here on King's Chamber. Something tells me that was not part of the plan, or else you would have been prepared for the animals. My intuition tells me there was something else you were supposed to collect, but did not find, so you decided to come here. I'll ask again, why are you here? What are you trying to find?"

Zahara's look of amusement substantiated the Master Chief's suspicions.

"Might as well get this over with." He nodded at the large, high-tech facility. "You'll find your answers in there."

Alston and Sorenson returned from combing through the northern side.

"There's nothing here," Alston said.

"Nothing living, at least." Sorenson was looking at the battered facility. "I'm not sure it's a good idea to go in there."

"Can't be any less safe than any other part of this island," Donovan said. He approached from the southwest side of the perimeter where the team arrived on site. Grezda was a few steps behind him. She was watching the jungle with her rifle at hip-level.

Kittner knew the body language. He walked over to the two snipers, leaving Zahara in Metwally's custody.

"You got a visual on one of those dinosaurs?" he asked. It was a question he never thought he would ask in a million years.

"No, sir," Donovan said. He handed his sniper rifle to the Master Chief and pointed to a grove of trees thirty yards out. "We have another visitor, though."

Kittner peered through the scope. Behind those crosshairs was the first of three bulky discs walking on eight legs. It was a visitor Kittner, Lewy, and Sadie were all too familiar with.

"Son of a bitch." He moved the scope slightly side-to-side and got a view of the other two crabs. The scratch marks on their shells resulting from gunfire confirmed they were the same ones he encountered earlier. “They followed us. You’d think those guys would be full by now.”

“They appear to be holding back,” Grezda said. “Not sure if they’re smarter than normal crabs, but I suspect they know we’re aware of them.”

“Great,” Sorenson whispered. “Maybe we should start a pot of boiling water.”

Kittner handed the rifle back to his lead sniper. “I want you, Grezda, and the cousins watching the perimeter. I’m going to check out the compound, make sure there’s no surprises inside.”

“Aye-aye, sir.”

Kittner moved to the compound with Herschel, Roach, Tajima, and Costa. Lewy and Sadie assembled at the door with them.

“Hope you don’t mind,” Lewy said. “I’m not too keen on waiting outside.”

Kittner nodded his approval. “Keep your head on a swivel. Either of you know how to fire a gun?”

Sadie tilted her head and made a “Meh” sound. “I mean, I’ve shot a few bolt-action rifles as a kid.” She elbowed Lewy. “But he’s an Australian *Rambo*. He should have no problem.”

Kittner looked to Lewy for confirmation. Then he saw the tattoo.

“Grezda, mind if we borrow your MP5?”

The sniper approached and handed her secondary weapon to Lewy. He checked the magazine, pulled back on the cocking lever, and switched the safety off. He was ready to go.

They entered the building through the south door and came into an atrium painted with blood. In the atrium was a wide stairway leading to the second floor. To the left and right were metal doors broken off their hinges, leading to a pathway to a large laboratory.

Kittner led a sweep of the area. The whole first floor was a large chemical and genetics laboratory. Throughout its hundred-foot length were a variety of workstations, complex machinery, storage centers, offices, cold storage rooms, and a hell of a lot of devastation. The northeast side had imploded inward from some kind of massive impact which broke down at least ten feet of wall.

Through the gap, they could see the damaged side of the dome and the huge footsteps leading up to the compound.

It was a sight that almost made Kittner ignore the find in the center of the lab.

A huge cube made of reinforced glass stood from a base made of metal and multifaceted machinery. Inside that glass was something Kittner could only describe as a large piece of rock. From the outside looking in, it appeared no different than any other piece of rock.

But Kittner, despite not being educated in the ways of science, understood protective measures when he saw them. There were mechanical arms, like a children's claw machine, hanging from the cube's ceiling, made for taking samples. All around the base were a series of supercomputers and monitoring systems.

"What the hell is this?" Herschel asked.

"A rock," Roach said. "What else does it look like?"

"They don't build a big containment unit for a regular piece of rock," Herschel said. "It's not uranium. There's residue on the bottom from where they drilled holes in it."

Kittner looked to the atrium as Metwally stepped inside with Zahara. Right then, it made sense.

"It's what he was looking for," he said. "He thought he would find it with the chemicals, but he didn't, so he decided to take a look over here. Probably would've been picked off with the rest of his men he had here had he not been distracted with the two of you." He gestured at Sadie and Lewy.

"What about that?" Lewy asked. He was pointing at the huge footprints outside the gap.

Kittner walked to the breach to investigate. The prints were the same shape as those made by the ceratosaurs, but larger. Kittner estimated they were eight feet long from the heel to the tip of the middle toe.

"Whatever made these is at least forty feet long. Maybe fifty," Kittner said. "Do ceratosaurs grow that big, Sadie?"

"Not to my knowledge," she said.

His eyes went to the dome and the massive fissure in its side. The people who ran this lab were dealing with forces they could not control, and it cost them their lives.

"You mean to tell me there's something *that* big walking around somewhere on this island?" Roach said.

"I want to go home and have beer," Herschel commented. "Lots of beer."

"Trust me, I'll be buying," Kittner replied. When he turned around, he saw Tajima studying a facility map on the wall. The merc, fluent in several Asian languages, studied the text marking each floor and room. His face contorted with a wave of confusion. "What does it say?"

"There's a greenhouse on the third floor," Tajima said.

The merc's confusion made sense. Everyone here knew this was not exactly the type of facility to store a greenhouse in. Usually, they would be their own separate building, not in a steel structure with no skylight.

They proceeded to the second floor.

There, they found a few lab rooms on the east side of the floor, with administrative offices and conference rooms on the west side. In addition, there were some private quarters for the head staff. Like the bottom floor, the entire area was trashed. The tile floor was torn up by clawed feet, the walls were full of craters and bullet holes, and every single office door was either unlatched or smashed open.

The creatures, in their rampage, were very thorough in slaying their captors.

Sadie moved to one of the offices and looked at the laptops on the desk. "Maybe we'll figure out what they were doing."

Kittner looked to Tajima. "You think you can hack into that thing and maybe find anything useful?"

"Hai."

"Good. Metwally, stay here with him and the trash," Kittner said. Metwally relished in his superiority over the prisoner with a sneering smile. Zahara gave him a glance, taking notice of his guard's attempt to intimidate him. True to form, the terrorist found the display more amusing than anything else.

Tajima opened the laptop and turned it on.

While he worked on that, the rest of the team moved to a large twisting staircase in the middle of the floor. At the top, they found the double doors open. A smell of something burnt and rotten assaulted their senses.

Guns pointed, they emerged and checked for hostiles. There was no movement on the floor, save for a breeze coming through a broken window.

Just as the map had indicated, the third floor was a massive greenhouse of sorts. It was not a conventional one for the growth of fresh vegetables in an isolated environment, but a whole other laboratory. The northeast corner was intact, the breach having been formed in the lower floors.

Four huge gardens with four-foot-high perimeter walls were placed on all four corners of the floor. All four gardens were a hundred-and-sixty square feet. Each one housed the wilted remains of a spherical-shaped plant in their centers. From the top of those perimeter walls was a bulletproof glass barrier that had connected to the ceiling. All four barriers had been shattered in at least one section, where vines, like enormous worms, stretched from the base of each plant into the lab.

Wired to each plant were a set of computers, monitoring their vitals as though they were hospital patients.

"More of these things," Herschel said.

"They were torched," Sadie said. "Look at the floor. The way it's marked up, I think it's fair to say the ceratosaurs took their killing spree up here."

"There are gas lines in each garden," Kittner said after completing a walkthrough of the greenhouse. "Sadie's right; the people running this lab deliberately torched them."

"I'd say to prevent themselves from becoming lunch," Herschel said. He knelt down and felt his pantleg where he had been snagged by the carnivorous plant near the beach. He looked at the indentations in the floor where the ceratosaurs stomped about. "Then again, why worry about that when you've got big lizards coming at ya?"

"Maybe this one has the answer," Lewy said. He gestured at the one by the northeast corner. The sphere had split apart, much like the one that nearly killed Herschel. In its core was a round base with pointed objects protruding upward. Their burns prevented the team from knowing their true colors and shape, but from what they could see, they resembled the seeds of a blooming dandelion.

"They didn't want them reproducing out of control," Kittner said. "Because of the dinosaur attack, the scientists knew they would not be able to contain these plants, whatever they are. So, they managed to deploy their containment protocol before they were ripped apart."

He was looking at some shredded and bloodied lab coats as he spoke. Whoever was wearing them had been completely consumed by the creatures in the days since the incident. Maybe they weren't working with noble intentions, but the people here at least had the honor to utilize their final agonizing moments preventing a potential widespread crisis.

"I know firsthand what these bulbs are capable of," Herschel said with disdain. "I'm glad they managed to torch the freaking things."

"Wait…" Roach pointed at all four gardens. "If they torched them, and there's no breach in the walls or ceiling, then where'd the one we saw earlier come from?"

The group stood silent, contemplating that question. Only one answer made sense.

There was a fifth plant on the premises. It was an answer which led directly to another question: Where was it?

Once again, Kittner's attention went to that strange dome thing.

"Donovan?" he said on the radio.

"Yes?"

"Are any of you available to inspect the interior of the dome?"

"I can. Crabs are still at the same spot."

"Copy that. Exercise extreme caution when checking the dome. You know that plant that nearly ate Herschel before the chopper crash?"

"Are you telling me there's another one?"

"Find out for me, will ya?"

"On it now."

Having seen everything he needed to in the greenhouse, Kittner went downstairs. Tajima was seated at a desk, sorting through several files on the administrator's computer.

"I'm guessing you've had some luck?"

Tajima nodded. "They've been busy."

The group gathered behind him and looked at the graphs and photos on the monitor. Tajima clicked on other windows he had pulled up, revealing long, detailed reports.

Roach smirked. "You were able to read all of that while we were upstairs?"

"I'm a fast reader," Tajima replied. "Unlike some of us, I don't spend my downtime scrolling idly through the internet."

"You'd be surprised what fun stuff you can find on the internet." Roach followed up the statement with a wink and a "ca-ching!"

Tajima stared aimlessly. He had seen many horrible things over the course of his career, but they all paled to the horror of the mental image intruding on his mind.

"Lay it out for us," Kittner said.

Tajima snapped out of it. "Right." He tapped a few keys and brought up the first document which outlined the basis of the facility's objective. "Where to begin? The place was staffed with geologists, geneticists, bio-engineers, botanists, chemists…"

"Just give us the short, laymen's version," Kittner said.

"The plant was extracted in Montana. Analysis of the soil and granite samples indicates it is over a hundred-and-fifty million years old. The sample they recovered was a dormant spore, cocooned in some kind of resin deep below the Earth's surface. It is carnivorous, using vines to snag prey and drag it into the bulb, where it entraps them and uses digestive juices to dissolve flesh."

Herschel swallowed. He felt the gravity of the fate he barely avoided earlier that day. Having lived a life of combat, he was no stranger to the risk of death. It was something he had grown to accept. One did not live this life without the daily possibility of getting shot, stabbed, or blown up.

But getting gradually melted while still alive was something else entirely.

"The specimen they found was a mature one," Tajima continued. "The larger they grow, the more area their roots and vines cover. Meaning, they catch more prey." He pulled up a 3D illustration of the plant's overall form. He put his finger to an underground sac underneath the main body. "This is where they produce their sap. That's what the people here were interested in. My understanding is it contains a potentially hazardous bacteria."

"That's what they were trying to weaponize," Kittner said. "Given the secrecy of this place, I'm willing to bet they had big plans for the stuff. Maybe sell it to somebody to use in war, or develop a treatment for the exposure."

"In that case, you could create a pandemic then emerge as 'the hero' when you present the cure," Sadie added.

"Very interesting," Roach said. "But how does that explain the giant dinosaurs and everything?"

The look Tajima gave him conveyed a clear message: *I'm getting to that. If you could just shut up for a second...*

"During the excavation of the specimen, multiple 'cocoons' were discovered buried with it. To sum it up, the sap the plant produces can preserve prey if it acquires too much."

Now it made sense.

"Well, holy gosh darn," Herschel muttered. "We've got super plant from hell! Not only does it act like a damn octopus, but it can place living things in stasis for millions of years."

"Was there a list of all animal specimens they had on the premises?" Kittner asked.

Tajima scrolled down.

"Four ceratosaurs, one Dimorphodon… aaaaannd… 'miscellaneous'."

Kittner's nose wrinkled. "Miscellaneous?"

"That's what it says," Tajima said. "The ceratosaurs were housed in separate containers. Probably those things outside." He pointed east to the steel structures near the compound.

"But there's only three of them," Lewy said. "You said there were *four* ceratosaurs."

"And there's nothing mentioned about whatever was in the dome?" Kittner asked.

"And what about the crabs and Davy Jones' pet?" Sadie added.

Tajima pursed his lips.

"Typical Americans," Zahara quipped. "You've got the attention span of a toddler."

A blow to the back of his head by Metwally brought him to his knees.

“Yeah, and the temper of one too, so I suggest you shut your mouth before I have a real tantrum.”

Zahara responded with a quiet laugh.

Kittner did not like it. He knew the scum was trying to get under their skin. Zahara probably figured if he was beaten, he would at least enjoy the satisfaction of his enemies going down with him.

“Hang on, I got something in the private messages this guy was sending out,” Tajima explained. “By the looks of it, they went to ship some product out from a dock on the south cove, not too far from where we came ashore.”

Kittner remembered the boat wreckage they saw before they were attacked by the giant octopus.

“There’s all sorts of warnings about risk of contamination,” Tajima continued.

“Contaminated with what?” Kittner said. “Toxins from the plants?”

Tajima reread the passage a few times, then double-checked some data from another window.

“No.” He brought up images of the rock sample they discovered on the first floor. “Contaminated by a sample taken from this.”

Metwally snorted. “A rock?”

“It’s not just any rock,” Tajima said. “It’s a fragment of a meteorite. Specifically, a broken-off portion of an exploded planet, according to the reports. The sample is developed from a highly hazardous material, similar to uranium. It can corrupt the DNA of anything it comes into contact with.”

“Whoa.” Herschel took a breath. The last piece of the puzzle was uncovered. “That explains why the big-ass tulips haven’t been discovered before. The meteorite landed in Montana and altered the form of some kind of prehistoric flora. It mutated into something big, and maybe due to some sort of seismic event, it was forced underground before it could spawn.”

“Wait, didn’t we see the one up there that was opened up?” Lewy asked, pointing upstairs. “You mean to tell me the original one did not spawn a bunch of times before it went dormant?”

Tajima went back to work sorting through the reports.

"Simple answer. They were extracting the seeds. Probably for their own method of incubation."

"Wow," Lewy said. "They were researching dinosaurs, killer plants, radioactive-ish meteorites, toxic sap. When the creatures escaped, some of the top brass here tried to make a Hail Mary attempt to get off the island with the product. Something chased them into the water and cut their trip short."

"It might explain why they were studying the dinosaurs," Sadie said. "If the original plant grew over the meteorite fragment, then maybe some of the animals it trapped may have been exposed to it when they were cocooned."

Kittner thought of the flying Dimorphodon. Now it made sense why it was so radically different than what the fossil record indicated.

"There's a lot of money in this project," Zahara said. "Who knows? My employer might double whatever you're being paid for capturing me. Maybe even triple, or *more.*" He looked at the mercenaries in hopes his efforts at tempting them were successful. "You're not angels. Don't pretend that you are. You do dirty jobs for the highest bidder. My men were being paid a significant sum. They're all dead, and we don't get paid until we deliver the goods. My client would be more than happy to provide those sums to you, should you join me." He looked at Kittner. "Maybe it would make the killing of what's-his-name from our first meeting worthwhile?"

Finally, Kittner snapped. A fist connected with the terrorist's jaw, knocking him down.

Instinctively, the Master Chief gripped his knife to permanently silence his captive. Seeing the look in Sadie's eyes brought him back to reality. For a second, she viewed him in the same horror as those creatures outside. Not that she had any sympathy for Zahara—nobody in their right mind would—but she knew what kind of damage a man of Kittner's ferocity was capable of.

He took a breath.

"Metwally, take the garbage outside."

The hillbilly teammate grabbed Zahara by the arm and yanked him to his feet. "Let's go, Lizard Bait." He pushed the terrorist to the stairs, not bothering to let him tend to his bleeding gums.

Kittner watched until the prisoner was no longer in sight. Even then, he found himself staring idly in the direction of the steps until Donovan's voice yanked him from his trance.

"Whoa! Chief?"

"Go ahead, Donovan," Kittner replied.

"You're gonna see some smoke coming out of the dome. We'll be using some of the fuel drums to start a flame. That plant that almost ate Herschel? There's a BIG one in the dome."

Kittner moved to the north wall and watched through a window as Donovan and the cousins moved drums of diesel fuel to the gap in the dome.

"Be careful," Kittner told him.

"Doing my best. And boss, in case you're not aware, I think there was more inside this dome than just another plant." Donovan was looking at the giant footprints as he spoke. *"Whatever made these were...eh..."*

"Fifty feet long at least," Kittner said for the second time. An ominous feeling gripped him as he looked beyond the perimeter.

He had a bad feeling of what became of that fourth Ceratosaurus.

CHAPTER 11

Metwally kept a firm hold on the prisoner as they stepped into the sunlight. Around the corner of the science building, the cousins were busy rolling a fuel drum towards the dome. Grezda was at the southeast corner, keeping tabs on the giant crustaceans wandering in the distance.

"Mercenaries with heart," Zahara quipped. "Out to save the world from an old plant."

Metwally tapped him with his gun muzzle. Zahara sniggered. That had been done so many times this day alone, not to mention all the other times in his life, that it had lost its intimidating effect.

"Might wanna shut up," Metwally said. "There's nothing for you to gain from this. You might think you're saving face, but all you're doing is looking foolish. We kicked your ass. You're captured. We're the winners here. I'm gonna go home smiling. You?" He chuckled. "You'll live a life where rice and beans will be considered a gourmet meal."

Zahara slowly turned to look him in the eye. He held that gaze, studying every millimeter of Metwally's features. His visual inspection went beyond a lookover of the mercenary's physical traits. He was looking deeper, connecting every twitch, expression, and word he had witnessed thus far.

"I'm not so sure you're gonna be smiling," Zahara said. "Even if things play out as you claim, I have a feeling you'll find yourself staring at the mirror, hating your existence." He nodded at the second floor of the science module. "I saw the way you perked up at the mention of a greater payday. That wasn't the look of someone who just likes to spend money." He leaned closer, his grin exposing the decaying, tobacco-stained teeth behind those lips. "You're a guy who needs a way out of a hole he has dug himself into. You owe somebody something, don't ya?"

"Shut up," Metwally said.

Contrary to his usual tone, the merc spoke with a shaky, unconvincing drawl. He sounded like a teenager caught in a lie who desperately wanted to maintain an image of confidence. For Zahara, he sounded like many people he had done business with. He knew the sound of a man at the end of his rope. Those were the people who were easiest to manipulate. All you had to do was offer salvation from the nagging situation that weighed them down.

For some, it was sanctuary from a pursuing force, whether it be government or a private hostile group who had been crossed. For others, it was the opposite; people who had been wronged but lacked the resources to do anything about it.

Then there were those who had buried themselves under a mountain of financial debt and could not climb out due to the steep interest rate.

Metwally was the third type, and Zahara knew it.

"What's your plan after this?" the terrorist asked. "Keep flying around doing odd jobs, all the while blowing it at the card table in hopes of tripling your money and paying off whoever quickly? Only to lose every single time, and face the wrath of the people you owe?" He nodded at the building; specifically, the secrets held within it. "Anyone caught in that scenario would be a fool not to take advantage of what my client is paying. And, as you are glad to point out, all my guys are dead. Meaning, there's a whole lot of wages that are going to be collected, but have nobody to receive them. Imagine all those wages from all those dead men, being given to one *stronger* and *smarter* man. A man with an eye for opportunity. It's a jackpot, and only a fool would look away from it."

Metwally closed his fist and readied to put the terrorist in the dirt. Like a force field, those words spoken by Zahara weakened his will to inflict bodily harm. After a few moments, he unclenched his fist.

Still hopeful in presenting an intimidating presence, he grabbed Zahara by the collar and pulled him close.

"You're full of shit."

Zahara's smile was unwavering. "I am many things, Mr. Metwally. But I am loyal to those who support my cause. How is it that so many people from all over the globe have joined the specters? There are so many freedom fighters out there, groups that would have been easier for my men to join. But they sought me out. Why? Because they believe in my cause, and I have never gone back on a deal. Even those who were once enemies were treated more than fairly when they crossed the line in the sand and joined forces with me."

Metwally inhaled through his nostrils. The angel and devil were on his shoulders, battling it out within his conscience.

"Even if I did entertain your bullshit, how would you even get us off this rock?" he asked. "Even if the rest of my team got eliminated, the ride Kittner has coming won't be so willing to go along with your idea."

Zahara tilted his head to glance at one of Metwally's vest pockets. "You have the SAT phone. Let me use it. I have an ally who can arrive here with some men on a seaplane. They'll get here long before Kittner's associate. They'll get here, we'll convince your people to arrive at the south dock where the Chinese had some boats, and give them a little surprise." He watched Metwally with unblinking eyes. The fact that the merc listened to every word spoken without interruption was a strong sign he was entertaining the proposal.

Metwally's grasp tightened. He could easily break the bastard's arms and legs right here, and the rest of the team would not complain too much. In fact, some might suggest they break Zahara's jaw just to ensure he stayed quiet. It would certainly prevent any further temptation.

On the other hand, Metwally was not sure if he viewed that temptation as a bad thing.

He reflected on his years with the team. Sure, they had each other's backs. There was never any bad blood between him and them. But at the same time, that word 'loyalty' stuck out to him. None of the guys offered to help him with his finances. It all started from trying to keep his younger brother out of prison for what he considered to be a bogus charge, then intensified when his wife divorced him and took everything including the ice cube trays from the freezer. Thanks to a good lawyer on her end and a crappy lawyer on Metwally's end, he was bamboozled into a five-hundred-grand alimony payment per year. Then there was the gambling which, as Zahara correctly guessed, was meant as a fast road to increasing his wealth. Instead, it only got him deeper than he could have ever imagined, and thanks to those damn interest rates—which were designed to keep people trapped—climbing out seemed impossible.

If anything, whenever his teammates brought it up, it was either in judgement or a cheap way to trash talk him. Loyalty was not something Metwally associated with these men.

His grasp on Zahara's collar loosened.

The terrorist stood up straight and waited silently for his new friend to pull out the SAT phone and dial the number he would provide.

"I don't know about you," Sorenson said to his cousin while they rolled the last barrel of fuel to the gap in the dome, "I have no intention of taking a single step in there."

Alston looked at the four other fuel drums they had brought to the dome with Donovan's help.

"What? You afraid one of those vines is going to snatch you up?"

Sorenson smacked his cousin on the back of the head. "Um, have you already forgotten what almost happened to Herschel? And that plant-thing was way smaller compared to *this*."

Alston observed the large bulb protruding on the far side of the dome. It was twice the size of the one they had seen earlier, and its brown vines had spread across the ground like tree roots. Those that extended outside through the breach were swiftly severed by the men's knives before they even began to worry about the fuel.

"Fair point," he said.

"Won't matter in a minute, anyway," Donovan said. "Get the marshmallows and the smoked sausages, because we're about to have a barbeque."

Both cousins backed away.

"No complaints here," Sorenson replied. He turned around and headed south along the east wall of the lab building. Alston trotted behind him.

"You're not gonna watch?"

"It's hot enough as it is," Sorenson said. "Besides, the plant is the least of our concerns." He looked over at Grezda. "How's it looking over there?"

"No changes," she called back. "The big dummies are hanging out in the same exact spot."

"Hmm." Sorenson looked at Alston. "A bit odd, isn't it? You'd think, if those things were on the hunt, they'd just move right in."

"Seems weird they'd come all this way just to stop at the last minute," Alston replied.

They resumed walking south.

"Who knows?" Sorenson said. "Maybe they realized we don't taste all that go—"

Alston stopped him and raised a finger to his lips. "Shh!"

Both men halted and stood silent. Sorenson sneered at his cousin, ready to berate him about shutting him up over nothing.

Then he heard it.

A voice, from around the corner, speaking some language neither of them recognized. But they knew the voice.

"The hell?" Sorenson slowly and silently moved in the direction of the sound. He turned the corner and stood in stunned silence, staring at his comrade, his brother in arms—Metwally—holding the team's only SAT phone up to the ear of their murderous prisoner, Zahara. The leader of the sadistic specter group spoke in some sort of Middle Eastern language.

Metwally looked past his prisoner-turned-ally, and paled after noticing the two cousins glaring at him.

His response was so stereotypical, they almost thought they were in a sitcom.

"I can explain…"

Sorenson, on the other hand, had veins verging on popping out of his neck and forehead. His dark skin took a different shade as the blood rushed to his face. White teeth bared, his usual nonchalant demeanor now a burning rage.

"You son of a—"

"Grezda? Grezda? Where the hell are you?"

The cousins turned around to the sight of Donovan rushing to the sniper's position. They moved to a better view, and before they could inform their teammate of Metwally's treachery, they beheld the sight of Grezda's rifle laying unattended in the dirt.

They shared a glance, still reeling from the gut punch of what they had just discovered. Revealing that info to the rest of the team would have to wait a minute, for Grezda's disappearance took top priority.

When they joined Donovan at her post, the sniper was inspecting the ground. There was a brief struggle, and the vegetation near the clearing had been bent out of their original shapes by a large, fast-moving mass.

Donovan put a hand to his ear and signaled to the cousins to be silent.

Together, they listened.

To the east were the sounds of movement; shaky, violent actions that ruffled the vegetation, dirt, and branches on the ground.

"Oh, my God." He sprinted ahead, speaking into his mic. "We've got contact. Southeast perimeter. Grezda's missing. We're going after her."

The cousins were right behind him, both keeping a watchful eye to the location the crabs were last seen.

After a hundred feet or so, they spotted a long tail, red and black in color, swinging back and forth like a kite string caught in high wind. The muscular frame of the beast it belonged to had crouched on those two powerful legs, its upper half driving all of its energy downward and side-to-side simultaneously.

Blood splattered in large red spurts.

The men moved in closer and spaced out to engage the threat. Lifting its head was an enormous reptilian, measuring approximately twenty feet from nose to tail. A horn protruded from its snout. Beneath it were a set of jaws where blood steadily dripped from. Two orange eyes with black pupils made visual contact with the mercenaries.

Despite everything they had seen up until now, the shock of what they were seeing hit devastatingly hard.

In front of them was a dinosaur. It matched the description their journalist friend Sadie Calis claimed she encountered.

Ceratosaurus.

The beast growled.

Under its chin was the brutalized corpse of Grezda. Her face was still, eyes bulging, tongue bitten off after having clamped her teeth in agony. Where her stomach used to be was a deep red crater, lined with the tips of rib bones.

"Son of a bitch!" Alston put his eye to the scope of his rifle, centering the electronic dot on the cerato's left eye. "Eat this."

A blur of motion swept in from his right.

SPLAT!

Blood rained over Sorenson and Donovan. They staggered backward, shocked by the apparition of red and black flesh passing in front of them, and the warm sensation of what was clearly blood.

They looked to the right where Alston was standing. He was still upright, quivering uncontrollably. The rifle fell from his hands, which spasmed from unruly muscular reflexes.

Between his shoulders was a stump, jetting blood a meter into the air like an unholy fountain.

"Christ!" Sorenson called out.

Another ceratosaur had decapitated his cousin and run off into the jungle. Before he could track its current position, the first one dropped its mouthful of Grezda's guts and came at them.

"Move!" Donovan said. He fired his submachine gun at the two-legged lizard. Bullets struck its thick skull, sparking pain.

Roaring, the beast pivoted on its heels. Its tail slashed high and wide, cutting through a couple of low-hanging branches before striking Donovan in the chest. The sniper was knocked several yards back, his secondary weapon firing wildly into the canopy.

Sorenson popped several shots, cursing in frustration as the surprisingly fast dinosaur sprinted into the maze of vegetation.

"This is Kittner. We're on our way!"

"Make it fast!" Sorenson replied. He tracked motion in the distance, catching a glimpse of the distinct skin color in the green background. Gritting his teeth, he followed the beast's motions through his rifle's scope. "Come on. Come get me, you…"

Remembering the tactic that got his cousin decapitated, he suddenly pivoted to the left and aimed in the direction the second ceratosaur had run off. As soon as he turned, it had emerged from behind some bushes, jaws wide, hot, rotten breath spewing from the back of its throat.

Sorenson popped off several rounds. A small drop of blood burst from its snout where a round impacted its thick skull. Shrieking, the beast veered left and pedaled its feet until it was out of sight.

"Cowards!" he shouted, rotating on his feet while sending multiple rounds in pursuit of the target. "You can dish it out, but you can't take it, can ya!"

The creature, as if directly responding, circled back and came at him. It stopped near the trunk of a large tree and watched the mercenary.

Sorenson adjusted his aim for a shot at its neck, only to freeze up after recognizing the sounds of rapidly approaching footsteps coming at him from *behind.*

There was no time to turn around and engage the enemy. The Ceratosaurus that had killed Grezda slammed its jaws shut over Sorenson's shoulder and pulled him backwards.

With a snarl, its brethren joined the action. Sorenson, his rear dragging over the dirt as he was pulled back, saw the second ceratosaur coming at him. Stricken by fear and adrenaline, all combat skills vanished from his mind, reducing him to kicking his feet at the second foe.

Undeterred by the pitiful defense, the beast lunged and closed its jaws… not over his legs, but his groin.

Sorenson looked to the heavens and screamed.

With Herschel, Tajima, Costa, and Roach behind him, Kittner raced from the research building. Metwally was standing near the southeast corner with the prisoner, looking uncharacteristically perplexed.

"They went over that way," he said, pointing to Grezda's post.

"Keep an eye on Zahara," Kittner replied. He looked at the entrance, at Sadie and Lewy. "You two stay here with Roach and Costa. Herschel, Tajima, on me!"

Without wasting time, they sprinted in the direction of bloodcurdling screams.

After tearing through a few dozen meters of wilderness, they arrived at a scene of horrific bloodshed. Grezda was on her back, her midsection forcefully removed from the rest of her body. Between her corpse and the team was the body of another teammate, who could not initially be identified as his head was gone entirely.

To the left was Donovan, laying on his back, his bulletproof vest slashed open. He was alive, but bleeding from where he had been struck.

Then there were the two beasts; ceratosaurs, playing tug of war with Sorenson.

The merc, spitting blood, let out one final scream before his anatomy gave way to the ungodly forces pulling him in opposite directions. His body separated at the waist, intestines stretching like electrical wires as the two dinosaurs backpedaled from one another.

Both ceratosaurs shook their half of the prize, savoring the taste of blood and relishing in the glory of the kill.

At once, they looked to the new arrivals.

"Oh, God," Herschel muttered.

The two dinosaurs were equal in size and nearly identical. The one clinging to Sorenson's upper body had a fresh scar running laterally down its snout, likely from a bullet skidding over its face. The other one had a chip in the tip of its horn; nothing that would impede its deadly nature.

Not that it mattered. The creatures were clearly more than happy to rely on their teeth to do their dirty work. And the look in those ugly eyes confirmed they were happy to add the new arrivals to the body count.

"Withdraw!" Kittner exclaimed.

The team unleashed a volley of gunfire, successfully repelling the dinosaurs. Tajima and Herschel linked arms around the injured Donovan and assisted him to the relative safety of the compound.

Kittner knelt by the body of the headless mercenary, whom he deduced to be Alston, and took his weapon. Duel-wielding assault rifles, he covered the retreat.

"Roach, get everyone inside," he said through the radio. "We've got incoming. Don't wait for…"

A sound of heavy footsteps approached from his ten o'clock.

Kittner directed both guns and sprayed bullets. The ceratosaur with the chipped horn came within view, performing a sharp turn as its thick flesh was pelted by the sharp lead. Unwilling to commit to the current attack, it raced eastward.

Another sound alarmed Kittner; something nobody in his profession wanted to hear.

"Oh, shit!"

Gunshots followed the exclamation by Herschel.

As Kittner sprinted through the perimeter, he spotted his three teammates making a run for one of the trailers. Coming at them from across the compound was the Ceratosaurus with the scar, having moved in a wide semi-circle to intercept them.

With no chance of reaching the research building, Herschel and Tajima dragged Donovan to one of the intact trailers. They made it inside with milliseconds to spare.

Herschel slammed the door shut, only for it to explode off its hinges after the Ceratosaurus made contact.

The beast whipped its head left and right, easily tearing through the door frames and widening the entrance.

A gunshot rang out, then a frantic scream from Herschel. The ceratosaur backed out of the trailer with the merc's rifle clenched between its teeth. Herschel's attempt to shoot the thing in the back of the throat had failed miserably.

Kittner looked over his shoulder. A howl from the jungle indicated the one with the chipped horn was prepping for another run at him.

It was no mystery how these creatures managed to overrun their captors. The ceratosaurs were agile and extremely tough. Not only that, but they were smart. They understood how to divide and conquer. In addition, they understood they could overwhelm their human foes psychologically.

Then there was the issue of their durability. While they were not impervious, it was evident it would take a hell of a lot of firepower to take them down. At this rate, given the chaos of the situation, the beasts would easily rampage through the team. A strategy was needed.

To do that, Kittner needed to buy time.

In the corner of his eye, he saw Grezda's sniper rifle. The purpose of her assignment came to mind.

The crabs.

For a crazy situation, might as well have a crazy solution.

He fired several rounds into the scar-faced Ceratosaurus. It scooted back from the stinging pain, then turned its eyes to the Master Chief.

"Come get me, sucker!"

Kittner ran as fast as his feet could carry him and prayed those big-ass crabs were still there. His life literally depended on it. He reckoned the crabs were not eager to encounter the dinosaurs, and probably had sensed they were nearby, hence they refrained from advancing on the compound.

He heard stomping feet coming from two different directions.

The diversion had worked. Both ceratosaurs were on his tail... and closing in fast.

Kittner pierced the terrain with his eyes in search of the enemy of his enemy.

"Where the hell are you?"

He cleared a patch of ferns then dug his heels into the ground to stop himself. Right in front of him was his answer.

Three crabs stood up on their armored legs and rotated to look at the lone human. Pincers clicked and eyes wavered on stalks. An easy meal had wandered over.

Rumbling footsteps grew louder.

Right away, the crabs spaced out, alerted to the approaching threat.

Kittner sprinted through the space between the crustaceans, narrowly avoiding the clutches of the third one's claws.

In the place he had stood a moment prior, the two ceratosaurs appeared. They exhaled through their nostrils and cocked their heads back, astonished at the armored blockade between them and their human prey.

The crabs, lacking the speed to escape the reptiles, resorted to offensive tactics. Arms raised high, their claws closing with loud snapping sounds. It was a display which failed to deter the dinosaurs. On the contrary, it only agitated them.

All attention shifted away from Kittner from both parties. Watching the bizarre event, he slowly circled to his right, monitoring the situation while searching for a clear avenue of escape.

The scar-faced ceratosaur lunged, head tucked down, bulldozing into the nearest crab. To Kittner's amazement, the crustacean flipped over as though light as a pancake. The ceratosaur moved over the fallen foe, head still tucked down. It tilted its body back on its legs, then brought all of its bodyweight down like a sledgehammer.

Bluish-green blood jetted from the crab's underbelly as the horn penetrated the relatively soft armor. Legs rotated in the air like boat oars, the claws attempting to reach the dinosaur's head, but lacking the necessary flexibility at the current angle.

Its stomach armor came apart under the wrath of the Ceratosaurus like crumbling paint. Rivers of blood spewed from the edges, carrying a foul odor that quickly permeated the air.

The Ceratosaurus with the chipped horn made a run at the second crab. Much like the first, it was knocked on its back, suffering a crack to its mandibles in the process. This ceratosaur performed the same attack, albeit with smaller and faster motions, jabbing its horn into the crab's underside with a woodpecker motion. Though it took a little longer, it did the trick.

The shell was breached and torn away, exposing the soft innards. Jaws ripped into the lungs and muscle tissue and munched it until the crab's insides were nothing more than chowder.

In spite of all logic, the third crab did not retreat. By now, it was fueled with its killer instinct. With its claws outstretched, it scurried to the second Ceratosaurus.

SNAP!

The theropod roared in agony, its left wrist caught in the vise-like grip of one of those pincers. It backed away, dragging the enemy's eight feet across the ground.

Sensing its sibling's pain, the scar-faced ceratosaur abandoned its recent kill and moved in to assist. The crustacean's legs had a wide spread, digging their pointed tips into the ground. A forward charge would not be as likely to topple the thing, especially with it holding onto the sibling.

The scar-faced dino went with a different tactic. It bit into one of the rear legs, lifted up, and twisted back and forth.

It took several attempts before the limb cracked at the joint. The beast pulled back, separating the limb from the rest of the crustacean.

The crab's free arm waved, unable to repel the second dinosaur and maintained its vicious grasp at the same time. It was a limitation that would cost it another leg in the course of the next thirty seconds.

All the while, Kittner made his way northwest, carefully monitoring the predators. The scar-faced crab had begun to tear off a third leg. By now, the crab had relinquished its hold on the other one's arm. Working together, the ceratosaurs wrestled their remaining opponent onto its back. It kicked its remaining legs in protest, helpless to do anything else while they proceeded to tear it apart.

The odor traveled as quickly as the Master Chief, permeating the compound.

When Kittner entered the clearing, he spotted his men gathering near the science building.

Sadie spotted him and alerted the others to his arrival.

"Oh, thank God," Herschel exclaimed.

"Didn't know you cared so much about me," Kittner said as he approached.

Herschel shrugged. "Well, you're in charge of the finances. Makes it a little harder to get paid if you bite the dust."

Kittner smiled and jabbed him in the arm. He then handed him Alston's rifle.

"I see you lost yours."

Herschel accepted the weapon. The moment turned somber, with the team grasping the reality that their numbers were drastically depleted. Grezda, Alston, and Sorenson were dead, and Donovan had suffered a severe injury.

"How is he?" Kittner asked Costa.

"I'm good," a groaning Donovan replied.

Kittner snorted. "Clearly."

Costa put a hand on her sweaty forehead. She, for one, did not find the situation funny at all.

She stood up and leaned close to Kittner to whisper in his ear. “He’s got a collapsed lung. The dinosaur’s tail was like a whip. It tore through his Kevlar and cut deep into his flesh. He’s losing a lot of blood.”

That last part was evident from the red puddle under the sniper, as well as his paling skin.

Kittner swallowed and tightened his jaw. It was the only outward sign of emotion he could allow himself. Being the team leader, it was imperative he maintained his composure at all times.

“We’ll get you out of here, Donovan. This place should have an infirmary.”

Donovan laughed, then coughed.

“Sorry, Chief. My number’s been dialed.” From his tone, the mercenary was good with his reality. It was a fate everyone in their profession risked. There was a good reason their pay was substantial. “Those things will be back shortly. Let me go out with a bang.”

He held up a few blocks of C-4.

Kittner shook his head. “I’m not giving up on you.”

Donovan’s face wrinkled. “Chief, I’ve never disobeyed an order from you. Don’t let me do it now.”

The blood spitting from his lips made Kittner accept the inevitable. He put a hand on the sniper’s shoulder. There was no point in asking if Donovan was sure. The guy was in considerable pain and wanted to get even.

“Give them hell.”

Donovan put a hand on his leader’s arm in response.

“With pleasure.”

CHAPTER 12

"You sure this'll work?" Sadie asked.

Kittner planted the last charge and stepped away from the dome. This was not a sort of tactic he was fond of using. Losing men was one thing. Sacrificing them was something else entirely. But this was Donovan's wish, and it was clear the guy was not going to make it.

Lewy and Herschel stood watch while Roach and Metwally kept tabs on the prisoner. Donovan was sipping on a flask full of whiskey. He usually drank it after the successful completion of a mission. For him, this would be exactly that, except he would not see the fruits of the labor.

"This will damn well work," he said on behalf of Kittner.

This was the most talkative the Master Chief had ever seen from the sniper.

"Donovan has not failed me yet," Kittner said. "I'm pretty sure he's got this."

"I seem to recall him failing you at one point," Costa said with a smile.

Kittner thought for a moment, then smiled after understanding what she was getting at.

"Oh, yes. The baked chicken incident. We survived two weeks of nonstop fighting in the Congo, barely getting a scratch, only to all get laid up from food poisoning." He looked at Sadie. "Be grateful you weren't there for that. Donovan's a hell of a shot, but he can't cook worth a damn."

"All of us except *him*," Costa added. "I guess he's exposed himself to his own poison enough that he's immune."

"What doesn't kill you makes you stronger," Donovan said with a weak chuckle, which quickly turned into a cough. The painkillers could only do so much against his severe injury. Costa had sewn him together the best she could and slowed the bleeding, granting him enough time to accomplish what he intended.

He took another swig from his flask, then handed it off to Kittner. It was a gesture known by many in the trade. When one's time was coming to an end, they often handed something off for safekeeping. In Donovan's case, it was the flask he carried.

The Master Chief took a whiff of whatever was in there and recoiled. He was a man who endured many foul smells, including the odor which still lingered from the recent crab massacre. Yet, whatever Donovan was drinking was enough to knock him on his ass.

"Jesus, Donovan. If your liver wasn't damaged from the dinosaur, I'd say it was doomed anyway."

Donovan smiled at that statement. "For me, a drink isn't strong enough unless it can be used as lighter fuel."

Kittner screwed the cap on and tucked it in a pocket. "Well, I hope you won't begrudge me refilling it with something a little more tame."

"Of all people, it's *you* who is the lightweight," the sniper quipped.

Kittner smiled. There was no better way of parting ways for the last time.

The timing proved to be perfect, as Tajima came racing from the southwest corner, grenade launcher in hand.

"We've got incoming."

"Both of them?" Kittner asked. Tajima nodded.

Costa took Sadie by the arm and led her over to the maintenance building. Given what they had in mind, it was probably not the best idea to hide in the research facility.

Lewy and Herschel, having heard Tajima's alert, moved in from the perimeter, both offering a quick and final salute to Donovan.

The sniper returned the gesture and watched as the men moved to the maintenance building.

He looked up at Kittner. "It's been a pleasure."

"Likewise," the Master Chief said.

Donovan cocked his head in the direction of Zahara, who was being escorted away by Roach and Metwally.

“No matter what happens, make sure that piece of shit doesn’t get away. I know the job was to bring him back alive, but frankly, I couldn’t care less. I just don’t want him to ride off into the sunset. The world is better off without freaks like Zahara.”

“That it is,” Kittner said.

“Don’t compromise anyone’s safety on his behalf. If you need to bust a cap in his skull, you do it, and don’t you dare lose a moment’s sleep.”

Kittner knew the sniper was not one for pep talks, nor was he normally the type to tell Kittner how to do things. He felt strongly about this issue, and the Master Chief was a man of his word.

“You got it.”

“Good.” Donovan unholstered his pistol. “Now, get out of here. I’m about to ring the dinner bell. You think that chicken dinner was bad? Wait till these dinosaurs see what I’ve got in store for them.”

Kittner smiled with pride at that statement. A true warrior, he admired Donovan for going out on his own terms.

And that was exactly what he planned to do.

He pointed his pistol skyward and waited for Kittner to get out of sight. Behind him was the breach in the dome, and the freakishly large plant resting inside of it. Its vines shifted in search of unsuspecting prey, each one lined with two-inch-long thorns.

All he needed to do was take a few steps back.

Footsteps approached. There was a banging sound at the trailer where he had taken refuge with Tajima and Herschel. The creatures were checking there first in hopes of finding the humans still hiding there.

“Looking for me?” He shook the air with numerous shots from his pistol. “Here I am.”

The tactic proved successful, with both ceratosaurs moving around the three containment trailers with haste. Their dark bodies, black as charcoal with red lines traveling across their flesh like highway lanes on a map, contrasted sharply with the fairly lush green background.

Both beasts laid eyes on him, their chins still wet from their gruesome encounter with the crabs. They stood side by side, taking notice of the large dome behind their target.

To Donovan's surprise, they did not advance on him right away. The beasts were prodding their snouts forward and taking whiffs of the air.

A ping of anxiety interrupted his confidence. Were they aware of the nature of the plants? Was this plan a big bust?

The one with the chipped horn growled and looked to the north. Its sibling with the scar took a step back, inspecting the ground with its nose.

All of a sudden, it made sense. They were picking up traces of whatever was being contained in this dome. As formidable as the two carnivores were, they weren't stupid. They only feared what they could not beat, and whatever was in here was well over twice their size.

Donovan felt himself growing weaker. The pain in his side was more than enough to overcome his painkillers. Lightheadedness was setting in. It was more than blood loss; it was his mind and body on the verge of failing.

Time was running out. And with that, his temper was coming to a boil. He wanted to die on his own terms, not sitting here uselessly while the two lizards stood and watched.

"Alright, this is getting boring." He extended his pistol at the carnivores. Three rounds struck the scarred one, and three more struck the other, all in the face.

All sense of apprehension had vanished in the blink of an eye.

The scarred one roared furiously, spewing saliva and God knows what else that was in its mouth in Donovan's direction. The one with the chipped horn moved forward with intent to take the first bite, only to be sideswiped by its sibling. The two beasts snapped their jaws at each other in competition, much to Donovan's amusement.

It provided him the perfect opportunity to move backward into the trap.

Vines shifted, detecting his presence.

He held the detonator in his left hand. "Bring it!"

The scarred one ended the squabble by successfully knocking the ceratosaur with the chipped horn onto the ground. Right away, it made its move, tearing through the opening in the dome, jaws wide to snatch Donovan up.

From that open mouth came a shriek. The beast rotated sharply to its right, its attention drawn to the numerous thorny vines coiling around its ankles. It tried to pull away, but failed to outmuscle the carnivorous vegetation.

The second cerato, believing its sibling's misfortune to be an opportunity for itself to snatch up the human, raced into the dome, only to find itself in the exact same predicament.

It squealed and stomped its feet, alarmed and agonized by the large tooth-like extensions coming from the strange tentacles.

Growling like a pair of rabid canines, both dinosaurs bit at the vines. More of them crept up their bodies, snagging their tails and necks. For every one they severed with their teeth, two more showed up.

Behind Donovan, the sphere peeled open in four huge petals. Inside was a deep dark throat leading to a stomach of sorts where prey was digested alive.

In his mind, the dinosaurs deserved such a fate for what they did to his teammates. However, in spite of their struggles, they were gradually freeing themselves of the restraints. In a few moments, they would be free to kill again.

Besides, what better final kill was there to put up on his scoreboard than two dinosaurs?

He extended the antenna on his detonator and put his thumb to the button.

"Time to join your ancestors."

The two ceratosaurs ceased their struggles and looked to the human, their sense of distress heightened, as though they knew their situation just got worse.

It did.

Donovan pressed down.

Kittner and his teammates tucked their heads down as the blast rocked the center of the island. Huge tremors swept under their knees, the roof raining dust on them. Pieces of the dome flew across the compound, trailing smoke. One large fragment came down atop one of the trailers, imploding the already fractured building on impact.

Tidal waves of dust and smoke consumed the maintenance building and those inside of it. The windows burst and pieces of the ceiling came down.

Slowly, the tremors ceased, the rumbles dissipated, and the suffocating clouds dispersed into the surrounding jungle.

Kittner looked up.

The first thing he saw was Sadie with her head down, eyes shut, while squeezing Lewy's hand tight enough to make the Aussie's face scowl. The woman had a hell of a grip. Regardless, he allowed her to seek comfort.

After a while, she opened her eyes and looked at the aftermath drifting past the open door.

"Wow." She looked over at Lewy. "You alright? You hurt?"

He faked a smile. "No. Not at all."

She realized what she had done and ripped her hand away. "Oh, my! I'm sorry."

This time, he genuinely smiled. "Nah, missy. You're alright. Though, I gotta say, you'd make a great iron worker." He looked up at Kittner. "Did it work?"

The Master Chief moved to the door. "Only one way to find out."

He stepped outside into the thinning cloud. A smell of plastic explosives and charred flesh traveled up his nose.

The rest of the group joined him outside and moved with caution to the blast zone.

Flames from the exploded fuel drums had spread far and wide. The northeast corner of the research building was heavily deformed, with large chunks of it blown away. What was still there was caked with burning fuel and marked by large metal shrapnel that once comprised the dome.

After moving up to the formerly large containment structure, the team gazed at the smoldering contents. What remained of the large plant was wilted and shrunken, quickly turning to ash.

One of the ceratosaurs had been launched all the way to the nearest container. Its body was more grey than black, for its skin was completely charred. Kittner was unable to tell which ceratosaur this one was, as the entire tip of its horn had broken off after it was thrown face-first against the structure.

The other one was already skeletal, having been standing near a pair of fuel drums, which had instantly ignited. One of its legs had detached from the rest of it and settled on the other side of the dome.

"Nice work, Donovan," Costa said, directing her voice to the heavens.

It was a bittersweet moment for the group. On the one hand, it was difficult to imagine Donovan no longer being with them. The same was true for the other fallen teammates. But Donovan was different, not in his value as a human being, but in the sense they all thought of him as unkillable. He was a crack shot with any weapon he had in his hands.

On the other hand, there was a sense of pride to be felt that his final act was in defeating their most formidable enemy so far.

"What now?" Lewy asked.

"We wait for our ride," Kittner said. "Probably isn't wise to wait here any longer. Not with the fire spreading."

They watched as some of the trees on the west side were consumed with flames. There was no way around it: a wildfire had been started, and nothing short of a torrential rainstorm would stop it. It would not be the end of life here on King's Chamber. Nature was designed to bounce back stronger than ever from such fires. The burnt vegetation would return stronger and greener than ever.

However, it did create a hell of a predicament for the team.

"I was able to check the map," Tajima said. "There's a dock on the south side of the island. Decent visibility. We can wait there until pickup arrives."

"We'll have to hope the fire doesn't get to us first," Roach said. "That being said, I don't see any other option."

"Nope," Kittner replied. "That's what we'll do."

"I'm just glad it's over," Sadie said.

A rumble from the north made her throat tighten.

Everyone froze, hoping it was a figment of their imagination.

A second rumble confirmed the opposite. As did the third, fourth, and fifth ones. Each vibration was stronger than its predecessor, and had a familiar rhythm to it. It was the same drumbeat made by the two ceratosaurs, except this time, it was louder.

Way louder.

Heavier.

Scarier.

The compressed stomachs and dry mouths all nine of them experienced, including Zahara, confirmed the latter.

A tree limb snapped free and crashed into the earth a few hundred feet back. After a few more footsteps, another one crashed down, having been torn from its rightful place by a colossal battering ram charging towards the complex.

The fiend emerged in the clearing. High and mighty, it was over sixty feet in body length—and that was not even including its massive tail. Its horn was gargantuan and terrifying in both its size and appearance. Unlike the triangular-shaped horns of its smaller counterparts, this one resembled something closer to that of a rhinoceros'.

Its skin was light grey in color, the claws on its fingers and toes long, narrow, and designed for slaughter. As deadly as they were, they nearly went unnoticed by the team, who were all focused on those colossal jaws.

Though different in its size, coloring, and horn formation, one thing was perfectly clear: this was a Ceratosaurus. Having been enhanced in both size and form by years of direct exposure to the extraterrestrial element inside the facility, it was now a titan that dwarfed even the most ferocious of theropods from its era.

"Holy God," Sadie muttered.

The reptilian tilted its head downward and lay eyes on the puny humans standing near the fire. Having taken part of the rampage which left all of the compound's original personnel dead, it understood the purpose of the firearms in their hands.

It cared little for their insignificant size. In the ceratosaur's mind, these people were not just food. They were challengers.

Kittner sensed this, as did everyone else in the team.

All at once, they opened fire.

The Ceratosaurus jolted from the sudden barrage of nearly invisible projectiles hitting it at the speed of sound. Its skin twitched, the light-armor-piercing rounds failing to even leave a scratch. Even sniper rounds from Costa's rifle failed to do anything but agitate the theropod.

It huffed and puffed, having been refamiliarized with the annoying stings after a few short seconds.

"This isn't working," Lewy said after draining the magazine for his MP5.

"No, it's not," Kittner replied. He looked at Tajima and his grenade launcher. "You waiting for permission or something?"

The merc took the hint and raised the muzzle. A squeeze of the trigger delivered the first of six explosives at the creature's chest. It exploded on impact, knocking the target backward. A second grenade struck the neck, and a third on its left hip.

Roaring in defiance, the dinosaur stomped through the cloud. On its hide was nothing more than minor scarring where the grenades had impacted.

A second bellow preceded its retaliation.

The team fanned out in different directions, except for Tajima, who stood with his grenade launcher pointed. Cursing the beast in his native language, he unleashed a fourth grenade.

It exploded over the cerato's face, doing little more than marginally slowing its assault.

Tajima pumped the launcher and stepped back in hopes of landing a shot in its open mouth. The beast proved faster in this instance, snatching up the Japanese mercenary and lifting him high in the sky. Jaws opened and closed in a munching motion, reducing Tajima's body to ground meat, while his arms, legs, and weapon fell from its mouth.

Spitting blood with its next roar, the beast turned to the sound of gunfire. Roach had backed up to the containment trailer, unloading his weapon at the creature's face in hopes of embedding a round in the soft eye tissue. A few of those shots came damn close, infuriating the Ceratosaurus all the more.

It rushed the flustered merc, who, in a rare display of panic, dropped his weapon and ran. He only cleared two steps before the beast closed the distance and plastered him into a three-toed crater.

Kittner, guiding the civilians to the north, watched in disgust as red strands of Roach stretched between the earth and the cerato's enormous foot as it made its next step.

Standing their ground was a death sentence. All they could hope for was to retreat.

He looked at the forest and the broken tree limbs left in the dinosaur's wake. If there was any advantage to its size, it was the fact it could not move through the island's interior without being slowed down by constant obstacles.

"Move! Move! Move!" he shouted to the others, pointing north with his thumb. "This way! Go! Go! Go!"

The six other surviving members of the group joined the Master Chief in his retreat. Behind them, the giant Ceratosaurus initiated its pursuit.

As Kittner had counted on, it had to force its way through some tree limbs in order to advance.

"Keep going!" Kittner shouted. He glanced to his right where Metwally was running with Zahara. He grabbed the prisoner by the neck and pulled him close. "What's up ahead?"

Feeling the rifle muzzle at his groin and hearing the booming footsteps behind him, Zahara was quick to answer.

"There's a rock formation a quarter mile that way. It's not exactly a mountain, but a long ridge overlooking the valley."

Kittner released him and resumed leading the team northward. "Then that's where we're going."

CHAPTER 13

Kittner felt an urge—a greater one than usual—to punch Zahara on the chin. While what the terrorist had told him was technically true, he probably could have mentioned something about the steep hills they had to ascend before reaching the large rock ridge.

Costa was constantly dabbing her face with a handkerchief to clear her eyes of sweat. She was at the front of the group, scoping the south with her sniper rifle in search of the Ceratosaurus. It had fallen back during the pursuit, partially due to the terrain, and a few sneaky maneuvers taken by the team in an effort to lose it.

"Any visual?" Kittner asked her.

She nodded. "Got some moving trees a few hundred yards back. It's still on to us."

"It probably has our scent," Sadie suggested. "It won't let up until we're dead."

Kittner looked to the south with bitter eyes. "Or until *it's* dead."

He took in the sight of the towering rock structure. Its tallest point had formed what was technically a cave, though it looked more like a cliff edge that was overextending to the south like an awning. The area above the ceiling was shaped like a crown, with pieces of rocks forming a miniature mountain range over the strange ridge.

That's a lot of weight for an area with limited structural support.

"What are you thinking, Chief?" Herschel asked, recognizing the look on Kittner's face.

"I…"

Kittner's thoughts were interrupted by the rapidly intensifying *stomps* from the Cerato's massive footsteps. Its pace had tripled, indicating it had found a break through the grove of trees.

Lewy heard it too. He rushed into the cave and frantically inspected it.

"There!" He pointed at a large gorge in the back wall. It was a fairly narrow split in the back wall, widening as it went farther into the ceiling. All the same, it was enough to fit all the team members. "We can hide in there."

There was no time to debate.

The group assembled, with Metwally and Zahara being the first to cram themselves into the tight space. Sadie and Lewy were next, with Costa right behind them.

Kittner looked over his shoulder. The treetops were swaying as the Ceratosaurus grazed past their trunks.

"Go!" He pushed Herschel in ahead of him, then stuffed himself into the gorge.

He had managed to scoot himself about five feet from the opening before those footsteps shook the ground underneath the ridge.

Everyone held their breath and went silent. Encased in darkness, and lit only by the light coming in through the ceiling, they watched through the sliver from whence they entered.

One moment, they saw wilderness on the other side. The next, they saw the rigid flesh of the bipedal reptilian.

It was in the cave, sniffing incessantly, detecting the humans, but unable to pinpoint their exact location. Holding its head low, it moved across the entire width of the cave, foot talons marring the rock floor.

After a few minutes, the view of the outside returned, with only the thing's long tail in their visual path.

"Forgive me for stating the obvious, sir," Costa whispered. "But I doubt we can do this forever."

"Maybe it'll go away," Metwally said. "We'll need to give it more than three minutes."

"Guys?" Zahara whispered.

Everyone, including Metwally, ignored the prisoner.

"Even if we do get out of here, it's bound to follow us to the south docks," Sadie said. "It found us with the corpses of the other two ceratosaurs, and it had spent its life in captivity. If you ask me, it does not have a positive view on humans."

"So, you're saying we're more than just food to that thing," Lewy stated.

Kittner bit his lip in frustration. "In that event, it's not going to leave anytime soon. Not if it has our scent."

Another moment of silence passed, during which everyone individually took in that statement as a reality.

"Then what do we do?" an impatient Metwally whispered. "Shooting our way out has been proven ineffective."

"The Chief had a plan right before we were rudely interrupted by our new friend," Lewy said. He looked over at Kittner. "What did you have in mind, sir."

For the second time, Zahara interrupted the group.

"Excuse me…"

The terrorist was fidgety, his eyes fixated on something on his right.

Once again, he was ignored.

Kittner studied the ceiling of the main part of the cave. "As Sadie had said, it has our scent. How 'bout we use ourselves as bait?"

Metwally swallowed. "And what exactly do you have in mind? Strap explosives to one of us and offer a sacrifice to the thing?"

"Tempting," Kittner said, eyeballing Zahara. "But I was thinking we bring the house down on it."

Everyone looked to the ridge extending overhead.

"It's worth a try," Lewy said. "I noticed signs of deterioration on the walls. If you guys have some C-4, we can make the chief's plan work. A few well-placed charges should easily get the job done."

"You think that'll work?" Metwally asked. "I mean, that thing can shrug off direct hits from a grenade launcher. You think some loose stones will mess up its day?"

"The rock up there has got to weigh a few tons at least," Kittner said. "We just need to find a way to distract the dinosaur long enough to plant the charges, then find a way to get it under the ridge long enough for use to detonate them."

Another moment of silence filled the gorge. After a while, it was Costa who rose her hand like a middle-school student. Not that Kittner could see through the darkness.

She leaned past Herschel to whisper in the Chief's ear.

"I hate to abandon our objective, sir, but we do have bait."

Kittner almost snorted at the suggestion. "Never thought you'd go that dark, Costa."

"Generally, no," she said. "But he is the leader of the Specters. And even though all of his crew are dead, don't think this guy won't rebuild his empire from the ground up. We don't know what our client has in store for him. For all we know, they'll let him go. Or just let him escape."

"Or use him for their own purposes," Herschel added. "The point is: we could easily use him as bait. I'm not excited about the idea either. But given the circumstances…"

"No!" Metwally said. His voice traveled through the gorge, sparking reactions from the others.

"For the love of all that is good and holy, Metwally!" Costa hissed.

"I know what you're talking about, and we're not doing it," Metwally said.

Kittner perked up.

Since when is Metwally, of all people, so concerned with high moral standards?

"Too many of our guys have died on this trip," Metwally continued. "I'd like to see the mission through. As planned."

Kittner gave consideration to his statement, then conceded with a nod.

"Alright."

"I appreciate your compassion," Zahara whispered, with no shortage of sarcasm in his voice. "But, again, if I may bring your attention to a larger issue. That is, if you'd like to survive long enough to drop rocks on the dino…"

Kittner could see the faint outline of the prisoner in the dim reach of the sunlight. He was frantically tilting his head to the right, deliberately bringing their attention to something deeper in the gorge.

In the next moment of silence, the sounds of something scraping against the walls of the gorge became apparent. After a few seconds, Kittner realized it was not 'something' but *many* somethings. And they were moving closer.

“Costa,” he said in an instructive tone.

Understanding what he wanted, she pulled out a flashlight and aimed it past Metwally and Zahara.

An eighth member of the group raised its ugly head. Mandibles, like pointed tongs, clipped against one another, while numerous spiky legs flailed from its elongated body.

It was red in color, sporting a long pair of antennae from its head, and dripped a continuous stream of saliva.

Sadie was the first to react. Not even the important purpose of their silence could prevent her instinctive reaction to such a sight. Nothing could—not when staring at a twelve-foot centipede.

She screamed.

Metwally shrieked and took aim with his rifle. Gunshots shook the inside of the cavern, resulting in ringing ears and a splotch of green fluid against the wall. The centipede reeled backward, its head carved open.

Huge stomps rocked the cave as the Ceratosaurus closed in on their position. It lowered its head and put its eye to the gorge, its pupil reflecting the glow of Costa’s torch.

A thunderous roar shook loose pieces of gravel from the wall.

Kittner leaned to his right as a gust of horrid breath threatened to knock him down.

“We’ve got a problem,” Metwally said.

“Good God,” Herschel exclaimed. “Y’all are on a roll with stating the obvious, aren’t you?”

“I’m not talking about the dinosaur,” Metwally said. He switched on his own flashlight and aimed it deep into the gorge. Behind the centipede’s still twisting body were seven or eight of its brethren.

An interruption in the sunlight from above made everyone look up.

As if their situation could not get any worse, another centipede uncoiled from a tunnel near the ceiling. The leg-span was maybe twelve feet, if not fourteen or fifteen. The length was many times that of the ones near the ground level.

Kittner’s jaw tensed. Not only were they trapped in here with a bunch of giant centipedes, but they had their *mother* to contend with.

“I think we now know what ‘miscellaneous’ meant on the databank,” Sadie muttered.

Kittner agreed with that statement. Those guys had to feed the Dimorphodon somehow. Why not breed their own food?

As it turned out, this gorge was not a convenient hiding place. It had formed when the mother centipede burrowed into the ridge and created its nest.

The smaller ones were closing in, completely unbothered by the death of their sibling. They traveled along the walls in straight lines, bringing out the entirety of their thirteen-foot lengths, as well as displaying their hundred legs.

They moved with frightening speed, leaving a trail of saliva in their wake. Razor sharp mandibles jittered, ready to bite into the soft flesh of the humans.

Kittner looked to the Cerato.

Its eye was still on the gorge, watching the humans.

Perfect.

He fired a single round from his rifle.

The Ceratosaurus recoiled from the gorge, its snout and horn grazing the top of the cave as it roared in immense pain.

“Go!”

Taking advantage of the Cerato’s misery, the team filed out through the opening of the gorge. Kittner took a right and led them along the back wall of the cave.

As Metwally and Zahara cleared the exit, the gigantic Ceratosaurus turned its head downward. A tiny river of blood streamed from its right eye, which, aside from the small wound, was still intact and functional. For that big monster, the rifle round was little more than the equivalent of a syringe needle to a human eye.

Its attention quickly turned to the small group of centipedes which came racing from the gorge. They took no notice of the gargantuan reptile as they pursued the humans. Good food was growing in short supply on this island, and they were not going to let some fresh meat evade them.

Nor would the Cerato. That, and it had a personal vendetta. First, it needed to rid itself of the competition.

The first centipede found itself crushed under its heel. The back half of the creature's body lurched, the legs frolicking.

Its seven companions were undeterred. If anything, they felt compelled to go after the Ceratosaurus itself. One of them scurried up its heel and dug its jaws into the tough flesh.

Nerves lit up in the dinosaur's leg. Its skin had not been breached, but those jaws were doing their best.

Another centipede joined in. Mandibles pinched the flesh around the ankle, slowly working their tips through the top layer of skin.

The mutant dinosaur shook its foot in a temper tantrum of futility. No matter how much force it stomped with, those pests would not shake loose.

Meanwhile, the others continued after the team.

Kittner took a glance back at them. Five centipedes were closing in on Metwally and Zahara.

He stopped abruptly and performed a one-eighty-degree turn. Dropping into a firing position, he signaled for the others to steer clear. The team fanned out, providing a clear line of fire.

Several rounds cut through the first centipede. Unlike the crabs, its armor was entirely insufficient against the onslaught from Modern Man's weaponry.

The rest of the team joined in, unloading their magazines into the other four multi-legged creatures. Green blood splattered, its color contrasting sharply against the brown and grey shades comprising the cave's structure.

Heavy tremors shook loose pebbles from various points in the big rock as the Ceratosaurus continued its outburst. A swing of its foot successfully flung one of the pests off. Its jaws were quick to clamp down on the bug, mashing it into a slop comprised of exoskeleton and guts.

The other one held on, digging in with both its mandibles and pointy legs. Infuriated, the dinosaur leaned on its left side and brought its right foot high. It kicked hard into the back wall of the cave and raked down in the same manner as someone scraping mud off their boot. Though not entirely shaken off, the centipede's grasp was loosened; enough so, that a concentrated downward swipe of the cerato's tail did the rest of the job.

Writhing on the ground like a nightcrawler, the centipede attempted to get its bearings, only to be pummeled into the earth by the dinosaur's mighty foot. The beast lifted its foot, then brought it down again. Then a third time, ridding the centipede of any identifiable remains.

"Damn!" Metwally exclaimed. "I'd say that was personal."

The Ceratosaurus released a puff of air from its nose, content in its revenge. It turned its eyes to the humans, who had foolishly not taken the opportunity to flee. Lips peeled back, its red gums dripped green centipede blood.

"Boss?" Herschel muttered.

Kittner watched the gorge. They had all seen the big one.

"Come on… come on out…"

The Ceratosaurus stepped forward and cocked its head back in a manner equivalent to a brawler pulling a punch.

Rocks fell from the high points in the ridge. A large fragment struck the Cerato's hip, shifting its focus from the humans to the source of the new disturbance.

There she was, the mother, furious and hungry. The upper half of her body extended from the highest point in the gorge, her legs tapping the ridge ceiling. She angled her head towards the Ceratosaurus and taunted it with a flaring hiss. There was no grudge held against the destruction of her offspring; given enough time, she probably would have eaten them herself. But the Ceratosaurus was a direct challenger in the food chain, as well as being an excellent supply of protein in itself.

The Ceratosaurus answered back with a rolling bellow, the vibration shaking more pebbles loose.

Tempers flared for another ten seconds, at the end of which, the centipede sprang into action. In a spring-loaded action, she launched herself from her perch and came down on the dinosaur. The reptilian howled as deadly mandibles pierced its neck and pointy legs prodded its hips, back, and underside.

"Who knows?" Zahara said. "Maybe she'll do the job for us."

The Ceratosaurus remained on its feet, clamping its jaws for a grip on the centipede's upper body. Lacking the leverage to secure a grip on anything vital, it cocked its body all the way to the left and focused on a section of the centipede on its hip. The jaws closed over a pair of the mother's legs and pulled them off. Green blood spewed from the open sockets, their owner shifting in considerable agony.

In spite of this, she proceeded with her attack, spilling scarlet rivers down the dinosaur's neck and shoulders.

The reptilian spun on its feet, slapping the rock wall with its tail. Its three-fingered arms thrashed, penetrating the mother's body segments with their nails. Still, she would not let up.

Kittner moved over to Costa and Herschel. "Give me all of your C-4."

Costa winced, knowing exactly what was on the Chief's mind. "Oh, geez, boss…"

"That's an order."

It was a rare use of a harsh tone from the Chief towards her, and it was enough to stow any urge to argue.

She and Herschel each gave him three blocks of C-4.

"We can help you," the latter said.

"I appreciate it," Kittner said as he armed the six blocks. "But I want you guys to get as far away as possible. This is my show."

"Are you sure there's nothing we can do?" Sadie asked.

Kittner opened his mouth to bark at them to leave. He held back, instead reaching into his top pocket and pulling out his last remaining cigar.

"You can hang on to this for me." He stuffed it in her hands. "If I pull this off, I'll fire that puppy up. Just take care of it for me in the meantime."

Sadie nodded. "I'm holding you to that."

The team turned around in unison and raced into the trees, leaving Kittner alone to do his duty.

He faced the two titans, who were still embraced in ferocious combat. The Ceratosaurus had successfully pulled off another pair of the mother's legs, and yet, she refused to release her grip. Furthermore, she shifted her lower body from its hips up to the dinosaur's back and stomach. The Ceratosaurus shrieked. In addition to the bites, she was constricting it like a python with a rodent.

A sense of panic took hold, and the beast charged into the cave wall. Kittner staggered backwards, half expecting the ceiling to come raining down on all of them. Though relatively weak in its structure, it was still holding firm.

The Ceratosaurus backpedaled out of the cave into the sunlight. Its enemy released her mandibles, only to inflict a whole new bite. The flood of pain caused the dinosaur to jolt.

In turn, it lost its balance and crashed to the ground. Legs kicked at the air, jaws biting nothing but air.

Kittner focused on the cave. It was clear now, enabling him to set the trap. He got right to work placing the charges at various points on the wall where the structure had the most damage.

"Chief!" Herschel said through the comm. *"This might not be necessary. The bug might get the job done, by the looks of it."*

Kittner looked over at the monsters. The Ceratosaurus was lost in a fit of madness, slapping its head and tail against the ground while the centipede continued dealing out her punishment.

"No. My money's still on the lizard. If the centipede doesn't kill it, it'll be back to pursuing us. We'll never get to the docks."

"Boss, it's out of the cave. You'll have to lure it back in."

"I'm well aware."

It was a half-truth. In actuality, Kittner was not sure how he was going to accomplish that particular aspect of the plan. For now, he remained concentrated on setting the explosives in the proper locations.

The Ceratosaurus shifted its body and managed to plant one foot on the ground. With a heavy push, it lifted itself upright, the centipede still maintaining her deadly grip.

After performing another useless spin, the Ceratosaurus steadied itself. Dripping blood from its neck and shoulders, it turned its attention to the nearest grove of trees. It was a moment of clarity for the beast, as it understood frantic action only played to the mother's strategy.

Some of those branches were hanging low enough and were plenty rigid to act as a brush. With this in mind, the Ceratosaurus charged at the vegetation, purposely plowing itself and its opponent into the wooden limbs.

Branches snapped, forming rigid spears. The Ceratosaurus continued pressing itself against the trees, allowing the branches to prod its own body as well as the centipede's.

Green blood spilled as the environmental weapon penetrated her shell.

A flux of nerve pain loosened her grip. Her jaws came loose and her upper body uncoiled in order to free herself from the spear that had been a simple tree branch moments ago.

The Ceratosaurus swung its head to the right, jaws opened a hundred-and-twenty degrees. With a sickening *CRUNCH*, they closed over the centipede's neck. Another hiss pierced the air. It was no battle cry; this was a shriek of pain and an awareness that the tide of the battle had shifted dramatically.

And it did.

With a single yanking motion, the Ceratosaurus whipped the enormous bug off of its body. Legs scratched its skin as she attempted to hang on, but the fierce motion proved too much. That, and the literal crushing pressure on her neck sent spasms throughout the rest of her body, making concerted action impossible.

The beast whipped its foe against the ground as though dusting a giant throw rug. Legs clawed uselessly, the body completely uncoiled and forming a groove in the ground.

As it had done with her young, the Ceratosaurus raised a foot, then stomped down hard on a segment of her body approximately ten meters from her head. The jaws tightened even further, jetting more blood from the breaches in her exoskeleton.

Mandibles clicked, then opened wide in a deathly spasm.

The Ceratosaurus twisted back and forth, pulling upward.

CRRRRAAAACCCKKK!

SPLAT!

Off came her head.

Kittner, waiting in the cave, prepped the detonator for the explosives while simultaneously keeping tabs on the brawl. His suspicion proved to be a reality.

"Oh, hell. Good thing we didn't place a bet," Herschel said.

"Damn!" Kittner replied. "I even thought of wagering five hundred bucks."

"Won't do you much good if you don't get out of there."

Kittner got to thinking. He needed to get the Ceratosaurus back in here long enough for the trap to work. All the while, he needed to get himself out. He was fine with self-sacrifice if the situation was necessary. As far as this case went, he was not convinced he needed to go that far.

He watched the mutant dinosaur. It stood triumphantly, sporting the severed head of its foe. Blood, both green and red, spilled down its body like a Christmas celebration from hell.

It had spent a lot of energy and was probably lacking coordination. Such conditions often led to clumsiness. All he needed to do was get the creature moving in the right direction.

He pulled a grenade from his vest.

"Crazy situations tend to require crazy solutions." After taking a breath, he pointed his gun at the dinosaur and hit it with half a magazine's worth of ammo. The Ceratosaurus dropped the centipede head and twitched from the barrage of pricking impacts. Looking at the source, it roared.

One of those huge feet kicked the centipede's body out of the way. Kittner released the lever of the grenade, igniting the fuse. The beast lowered its head and pedaled its legs, charging headfirst into the cave.

Kittner chucked the grenade, then turned to the right and ran as fast as his legs could carry him.

The grenade struck the creature's face.

BOOM!

Blinded by the concussive force and unable to stop its own momentum, the Ceratosaurus plowed against the cave wall. Its back half lifted off the ground from the impact, and the beast collapsed on its side.

It lifted its head, grunting and snorting, its senses warped from two consecutive hits.

Kittner exited the cave and reached the nearest trees. There, the team was waiting, having refused to leave him behind.

"Holy shit," a dumbfounded Metwally said.

Kittner, breathing heavily, held up the detonator. "What can I say? Sometimes, I amaze even myself."

He pressed the button.

Six explosions rocked the inside of the cave, spewing a thick cloud of dust into the trees.

A rumbling sound traveled up the height of the ridge as the rocks comprising the structure cracked and separated. A few pieces fell free, then some larger ones.

Then, all at once, the entire crest came apart. Thousands of pounds of granite collapsed on the struggling Ceratosaurus.

The team held their position, holding their breaths to avoid breathing in the dirty air. It took a minute or two for the cloud to dissipate enough for them to get a visual of the aftermath.

All they could see was a gigantic pile of rock. No dinosaur. No movement.

Now, everyone could breathe easy.

"Please tell me it's dead," Sadie said.

"Wanna dig it up and find out?" Lewy joked. She jabbed him in the ribs, sparking laughter from the others.

"I think I'm willing to roll the dice," Metwally said. "Let's get the hell out of here. I've had enough of this freaking island."

"That I can agree with," Kittner said. "But first…" He held his hand out to Sadie. Smiling, she planted the cigar on his palm.

Kittner lit it up and took a nice long draw.

"Tastes like victory."

It was a luxury he planned to take full advantage of. After all, they had a long walk ahead of them.

CHAPTER 14

The walk was long and hard. Avoiding the forest fire did not help matters. The flames started by the explosion in the dome were spreading fast and showing no signs of stopping. Like an invading army, the flames expanded in all directions, consuming anything in its path, wiping out all life on the island. Soon, a barren wasteland would be left behind, which would soon sprout new life from the ashes, as Nature had designed it.

"I hate to be that person," Costa said, "but are we almost there?"

"What's the matter?" Herschel asked. "Are your feet sore?"

"As a matter of fact, yes!" she replied.

Sadie stopped and lifted one of her feet to give it a moment of relief. "You're not alone."

Lewy took her by the arm and helped her along. "Yes, we're almost there. I think I can hear breakers."

"Same," Kittner added. His cigar was burnt to the stub. He took his last draw and stomped it into the dirt. "I already could go for another."

"I, for one, could use a drink," Lewy said.

Sadie giggled. "Same." She hobbled alongside him, her feet feeling as though they would fall off at any moment. All the while, she kept glancing at her charter, appreciative of the nonstop assistance he provided even after losing his boat. "Sorry about your yacht."

"Hmm?"

"I said I'm sorry about your yacht," she repeated. "Had I known the hazards surrounding this place, I probably wouldn't have gotten you involved."

Lewy chuckled. "Ah, yes. Shame on you. How dare you not know a super-sized octopus was lurking off the shores of this island?"

"That, and flying reptiles," Herschel added.

"Right?" Costa chimed in. "Not to mention big man-eating plants."

"And a big, angry, mutant Ceratosaurus," Kittner said.

Uplifted by the banter, the team pressed on. Smoke drifted southwards, carrying heat from the flames which spawned it. The breeze was not helping matters. It would not be too long before some satellite detected the event. Nothing would be done, as the island was uninhabited, and it would be too much of a drain on resources for no real gain.

A series of heavy rumbles from the north brought the group to a silent pause. They looked in that direction, weapons ready.

It was a sound that was too familiar.

"It *is* dead, right?" Lewy asked.

"Wanna go back and find out?" Sadie quipped. That got her a cockeyed glance from the former yacht captain.

"You're a real charmer, aren't you?"

They waited for another minute, during which no other sounds were heard.

"The fire's not too far back," Herschel said. "Maybe falling branches."

Lewy grimaced at a thick whiff of smoke wafting in his face. "As if this job wasn't shitty enough."

"Hopefully, she paid you well, Lewy," Costa said. "Unless I'm mistaken, this'll probably be your last charter for a while."

"I could argue for a discounted price," Sadie joked. "After all, the deal was for him to take me here and back. Technically, only half the bargain was met."

"Oh, you're a real charmer," Lewy said. "No, I think I'm ready to move on to different ventures."

"You could own a new charter business. Maybe flying." She beamed a smile at him. "At least, that way, you won't have to worry about giant octopuses."

Lewy grinned. "That's very true."

"Besides, if I'm going to pursue a career in investigative journalism, I'll need someone to get me from point A to point B," she continued.

Lewy stopped and looked her in the eye. There was a hidden meaning behind those words; something with deep feeling. For the first time since the service, someone was willing to have their life put in his hands.

Kittner tried to hide his childlike smile. *Dude, just kiss her already. Damn!*

The levity was stripped away by a blur of motion from behind the trunk of a tree. It was maybe twenty meters to his two o'clock, and though he only saw it for a millisecond, Kittner knew that was no dinosaur.

He knew that kind of movement all too well—someone was watching them and trying to remain hidden.

"Hold up." His sharp whisper successfully got the group's attention. He looked to Herschel and Costa. "Get near the friendlies. Metwally, put a gun to Zahara's head. We're not alone."

"No, you're not," Zahara said. The confidence in his tone spoke volumes in itself.

Kittner turned around.

Lewy's hands were up. Pressed to the back of his head was the muzzle of a pistol, held by no other than Zahara himself. To his left stood Metwally, pressing his rifle muzzle between Sadie's shoulder blades.

Herschel and Costa turned to face them, alarmed by the sudden turn in events, and disgusted by the betrayal by their so-called brother-in-arms.

"Metwally," Herschel groaned. "You son of a bitch."

"How could you do this?" Costa asked. Her eyes were on the verge of watering. The worst thing about betrayal was that it never came from an enemy. Metwally was never the most charming of fellas, but she never thought in a million years that he would stoop to this level.

They had been all over the globe together. On plenty of occasions, they had saved each other's asses.

After everything, Metwally was able to reduce his team members to mere obstacles to a bigger paycheck. And everyone knew, even before Metwally could say anything, that the answer to her question was exactly that: a bigger paycheck.

Zahara whistled loudly, an obvious signal to whomever was out there.

Kittner looked to the southwest where he had got a glimpse of one of the men. Slowly, a man in camouflage clothing stepped from behind the tree. In his hand was an AK-47.

Another appeared east of their position, with two more emerging directly from the south. A fifth and sixth arrived from the west, all holding automatic rifles. All of them wore military-type gear, with the exception of one of the guys approaching from the south, who sported a white shirt and jeans.

"Parsons," Zahara said to him. "Glad to see you made it."

"Zahara," the man named Parsons replied. "You better have that money you promised. Getting here on such short notice was not the easiest thing to do. Especially sharing my plane with your friends."

One of the paramilitary guys belched.

Zahara turned his gaze to Kittner and grated his nerves with a devious smile. "Should've killed me when you had the chance."

Kittner was not sure who he hated more at this moment: Zahara or Metwally.

"Now I see why you were so eager to speak up for him back at the cave," he said to the latter. "How much is he promising to pay you?"

"More than you ever have," Metwally responded. There was no emotion in his voice aside from a tinge of bitterness. He was a man who had resigned his soul and his conscience in favor of a fast solution to problems he created for himself. Problems he, knowing his habit, would probably revive in the upcoming years.

"More than we have?" Kittner said. "How about loyalty? You always had that from us. You think you'll get that anywhere else? From guys like him?" He jerked his head over at Zahara.

Metwally looked up and smiled, as if he was a high school student mocking an instructor during a 'do better' speech. Nothing Kittner said was getting through, or if it was, he was forcibly removing it from his consciousness.

"Can't pay bills with loyalty," he said. "Sorry, Chief. We're mercenaries. We work for the highest bidder. Don't act like we're angels."

"Oh, shut up," Herschel said. "Nobody ever made such a claim. But we're not monsters either. And we don't use our friends to make a quick buck."

"Kittner saved your ass on how many occasions?" Costa added. "Including today at the rock. You'd be halfway to being dinosaur shit right now if he didn't stay behind."

"Thanks a bunch," Metwally said. "But, like I said, I work for the highest bidder. That's the way it's going to be."

"Spoken like a wise man," Zahara said. "First thing's first: Drop your guns. Or else, your new friends will be the first to die."

Kittner, Costa, and Herschel kept their weapons on the terrorist leader. It was the only thing keeping the posse from unloading on them. Even with Lewy being used as a human shield, all they would have to do was unload, and Zahara would be toast. In that event, Lewy would be a dead man no matter what they did. The threat to Zahara's life was the only card they had at their disposal.

"You really don't listen good, do ya?" Metwally said.

Kittner scoffed at his former teammate. "Same could be said for you." He watched Metwally give an open-mouth smile, astounded by what could possibly be meant by that statement.

Sadie, on the other hand, tilted her head left, listening to another faint rumbling sound coming from the north.

Perhaps there was a way out of this. All they needed to do was stall. With that in mind, she went for the tactic she knew best.

"Like you aren't planning to kill us anyway," Sadie said in an indifferent, borderline sarcastic tone of voice. "You know guys like Zahara. If they're not shooting something, they're not having a good day. I imagine on Christmas morning, he hopes to find a new bomb under his tree. Or a gun. And if it comes with someone to shoot, all the better."

Lewy glared at her. It was a look that spoke a thousand words, all with the meaning of *Um, what the hell are you doing?* Beyond that, there was his fascination with her defense mechanism of humor. Just like before, she displayed a tendency to deal out some wit whenever she was held at gunpoint.

"You really don't understand how hostage situations are supposed to work, do you?"

She looked over at him. "What? Am I supposed to cry?"

"Probably be better if you said nothing," he replied.

"Oh, yes. That's exactly what these guys would like," she said. "Let's be real: do I really want to be taken alive by scum like these? We know what they probably do to female captives."

"And you think flapping your gums will better your odds?" Lewy said.

"It might get the thing done faster," she replied. "I can talk up a storm and drive a fella so insane, he'd consider risking life in prison just to shut me up."

Lewy sneered. "Can't deny that."

"Fortunately, for these guys, they won't have to worry about such laws. They're out here in the middle of nowhere, on an island where prehistoric plants grow, and mutant dinosaurs and other creatures roam."

The man named Parsons raised his eyebrows and looked to Zahara.

"Dinosaurs?"

Sadie looked at him. "Yeah, schmuck. Don't you know this place is practically *The Lost World?* Except, these monsters aren't made from crappy CGI or hand puppets. Ask your boss. He'll tell you all about them."

Parsons kept his eyes on Zahara. "What?"

Right them, it became apparent that Zahara had not mentioned the mutations when he placed the call. Not even a man of his stature would be taken seriously if he started making claims about prehistoric predators.

Zahara's usual sense of self-control was quickly waning. He had his captors at gunpoint and was on the edge of victory, but yet everyone was fixated on this bullshit.

"How about we talk about this later?" he said.

"Why not now?" Sadie said. "Can't you see he's curious?"

Parsons started to chuckle. He certainly did not expect the standoff to result in bickering about dinosaurs.

His eyes went to Zahara again. "You know, you dumb shits could've avoided this altogether if you just shot these guys in the back when you had the chance. Instead, you had to do the 'movie villain' thing of having to take a hostage."

"Oh!" Sadie raised a finger to get their attention. "About those dinosaurs…"

Parsons groaned. "Will you shut up about the damn dinosaurs? Jesus, lady!"

She shrugged. "Suit yourself."

"What could possibly be so important about fucking dinosaurs that you have to bring it up while you have a gun to your head?" Parsons said.

Sadie nudged her head backwards. "Probably because you're about to see one. We hoped we had killed it, but judging by those footsteps behind me, it's up and running… and still has our scent."

Everyone went quiet and listened to the rampant drumming of *STOMP! STOMP! STOMP!*

A tree toppled over, making way for a very pissed off and scarred Ceratosaurus. Its neck and hide bore the markings of its recent conflict with the centipede mother, as well as numerous lacerations and contusions received from the collapsed cave ceiling.

Furious and in considerable pain, the beast towered over its smaller foes. There was a hint of perplexity in its eyes, probably in response to the discovery of more humans added to the group.

For the creature, they were no real issue. If anything, they were extra protein, and an added source of satisfaction for its perpetual urge to kill.

As expected, Zahara's band of gunmen shifted their attention from their intended targets to the gargantuan new player. Panic set in for some, while others were naturally constricted by the utter shock from what they were seeing.

Both reactions led to the same response from all of them—gunfire.

The Ceratosaurus sneered. This time, it did not even flinch at the onslaught of annoying bullets. It just went for the kill.

Lunging forward, it swept its jaws downward in a golf-swing motion. The gunman in their path put his hands up and spent his last milliseconds letting out a high-pitched scream.

A puff of red mist spewed from the corners of the dinosaur's mouth. In the following moment, body parts rained down onto where he last stood.

The posse dispersed in an effort to both avoid and take down the predator. Hundreds of bullets pelted its thick skin, leaving the shooters enraged at the lack of damage being inflicted.

Zahara and Metwally grew antsy, their eyes shifting between the dinosaur, to the surrounding chaos, and Kittner.

He was sweating. Truly, he had lost control of the situation.

His sense of defeat was solidified as he watched Parsons attempt to make a run for the south beach. Seeing him, the Ceratosaurus moved in. A huge shadow encompassed the seaplane pilot, causing him to look straight up. Above him was the back of the creature's throat.

"AGH!"

SNAP!

The Ceratosaurus lifted its head. Sticking out from its front teeth were Parson's legs, still kicking, his screams muffled by its mouth.

Added pressure separated those legs from the rest of him, and a *GULP* delivered everything else into its stomach.

The terrorist, being a fast thinker, wrapped his arm around Lewy's neck. He looked at Metwally.

"Come on!"

The traitor took hold of Sadie in the same manner and followed his new boss westward.

Before Kittner could issue a warning, he and the others were forced to dive out of the Cerato's path.

Kittner went south while Herschel and Costa went north. The beast passed between them, missing Kittner with its jaws. It continued onward in pursuit of one of the other posse members.

As it did, its tail slashed to the right.

Costa yelled out and hit the ground. Herschel stopped and turned around, finding the sniper lying on the ground and the tip of the tail zipping past her. The monster took no notice of the fallen mercenary, as it was busy crunching the gunman between its teeth.

Kittner double-backed and joined up with them, dropping to one knee after reaching Costa. She was gasping for breath, the pain immediate and overwhelming.

"I think I did more than slip a disc," she managed to quip.

"That you did," Kittner said. "Can you move your legs?"

She tried, then shook her head.

"Looks like surgery is in her future," Herschel said.

"And maybe retirement," she added, keeping up an upbeat attitude behind the veil of pain.

"First, we need to get off this island. Fortunately, we have a ride." Kittner looked in the direction where Zahara and Metwally had gone with Sadie and Lewy. "And a pilot."

The Ceratosaurus performed a three-hundred-and-sixty-degree turn, giving its tail deadly momentum. It struck another one of the gunmen, exploding his body on impact.

Two others were left. Now realizing the futility of their weapons, they decided to make a run for it. With the dinosaur blocking their path to the beach, they turned tail and ran north. Prioritizing those who had actually tried to put up a fight, it gladly pursued, leaving the three mercenaries alone for now. As far as it knew, they had nowhere to run anyway.

"Get her to the beach," Kittner told Herschel. "Now!"

Herschel scooped Costa off the ground like a groom carrying off his bride. Even with all the pain she was in, Costa just had to smirk at the interesting dynamic.

"Don't get any ideas," he said to her.

They went south and Kittner went west.

Unhindered by hostages, the Master Chief was able to close the distance very quickly. He could hear Metwally bickering with Sadie while she struggled against his exertions.

"I swear, if you don't walk, I'll bust a cap in your forehead!"

"Yeah?" she shot back. "And how else will you get Captain Australia to fly the plane?"

"I can think of—"

All four of them turned around and laid eyes on Kittner. He came to a sudden stop, let his rifle hang by its strap, and held up two grenades. Their pins dangled from his thumbs, the levers held in place only by his grips.

"It's over, Zahara."

"For you, it is!" the terrorist replied.

All five of them listened to the bloodcurdling howls of the last two of the rescue team as the Ceratosaurus made good on its murderous instincts. One of those screams ended with a *STOMP* and a "BLECH!" The other fired off a few shots, then squealed as some branches snapped, as did all of his bones in a surreal *CRUNCH* sound.

Zahara and Metwally stood side-by-side, each using a prisoner as a human shield.

Kittner's gaze was sharp, analyzing every aspect of the situation, including the environment around them. The heat of the flames was carried in the breeze, as was some suffocating smoke.

The green leaves were starting to turn grey as ash clung to them. Several plants to the north were already starting to coil as they succumbed to the worsening conditions.

One particular plant shifted along the ground like a dying snake. Kittner paid close attention to its texture and location. If God was on his side, he was throwing Kittner and his friends a lifeline at this very moment.

"Seems like we're in quite the pickle," he said. "The way things are going, neither of us are going to make it off this island. So, how about we adopt Metwally's philosophy?"

His two enemies furrowed their brows.

"The hell you talking about?" Metwally said.

"I'm saying, why don't we *all* get on that plane?" Kittner said. "No sense in staying true to values if they're just gonna get you killed. Either we're going to get eaten by that thing, or we'll get cooked in the forest fire. Neither sound good to me. I'd rather get out of here and get paid. If we have to join forces with the guy we were hunting, then that's what we'll have to do. Like you said, Metwally, we're mercenaries. We're not angels."

Lewy, playing to the Chief's strategy, started nodding incessantly. "Yeah… if all of you drop your weapons and work together, I'll fly everyone out of here."

"Time's a-wast'n," Sadie said. "Sounds like a reasonable deal to me."

Zahara stood still as a statue. He was mostly certain the promise was an act, but he was making the critical error of listening to the ten percent of his mind that considered it to be true.

Metwally, however, was having none of it.

"Oh, for chrissake! He'll *never* let you off this island!"

"Shut up," Zahara said through bared teeth.

"Let's just shoot him," Metwally whispered in a pitiful attempt to go unheard by Kittner.

"Shut up! I need to think!"

With all of his plans having gone sideways, Zahara was lost in the confusion that came from a complete lack of control. He couldn't shoot the Master Chief, as he was smart enough to know those grenades would come his way, hostages be damned. Kittner was not generally one to sacrifice people, but he was also able to do the math, and he knew Lewy and Sadie would not see the light of day after outliving their usefulness. Killing the hostages would also get him nowhere. It was lucky enough that Lewy had the knowhow to fly small planes.

Zahara was an extremist, but he was not an idealist. He had no intention of dying for the cause; that part was best done by other people, in his opinion.

The ground shook as the Ceratosaurus started moving in their direction.

"We don't have time," Metwally said. "Let's move!"

"Wait," Zahara whispered.

Metwally shook his head. "Back off, Kittner. Back off, or I shoot the lady!"

Kittner held his ground.

Metwally pushed Sadie forward and put his rifle muzzle to the back of her head. "Then kiss her ass goodbye!"

BANG!

Metwally lowered his gun and stumbled backward. Blood spat from his mouth and jetted from the big hole in his throat. He tried to take a breath, but only filled his lungs with his own blood.

He looked over at Zahara, who stood pointing the very handgun the traitor had given him after removing his restraints. A giant blood bubble extended from his mouth. Metwally was a dead man—killed by the very guy he had betrayed his team for.

As that thought reached its conclusion, so did his life.

Zahara watched his situational ally fall to the ground. He took a breath, still grappling with the idea of forging an alliance with Kittner. The ever-approaching footsteps did not grant him an opportunity to think.

Before he could begin to make peace talks, an object struck the ground near his foot. It was a spherical object, made of metal.

A grenade!

"You double-crossing…"

Zahara scooted backward, nearly tripping over his own feet. He made nearly five yards of distance before he realized one critical factor: the lever was still attached.

The pin had been replaced. Kittner had thrown an untriggered grenade.

He took a breath and sneered at the Master Chief. "What's the big idea?"

Kittner shrugged. "Just needed you to back up."

As soon as he heard those words, Zahara felt something corkscrewing around his leg. It was a light sensation at first, but in the blink of an eye, it contracted with bone-crushing force.

Next thing he knew, his foot was yanked out from under him. Zahara landed on his back and was pulled northwest over the ground. Small ferns smacked his face like medieval peasants abusing a prisoner sentenced to death on his way to the headsman.

Zahara yelped, both from the abuse, and from the deep thorns burrowing into his thigh and calf.

By then, he realized he had played right into Kittner's plan—he had backed straight into the reach of a pod's tentacles.

Just as Metwally had met his end by crossing a line and betraying the team, Zahara met his by crossing his own line and trying to join forces for a common goal.

"Kittner! You bastard!"

The Master Chief joined up with the two friendlies and watched the tentacle vine drag the terrorist to the large spherical plant. The orb came apart in four large petals. Zahara threw his hands about, grabbing anything he could. What he did seize failed to keep him from his doom.

"NO!"

He was pulled into the base of the plant. There, a small fissure opened up, leading to an esophagus of sorts, where he was slurped. The petals closed up, completing the process of entrapment.

Next was the process of digestion. All without the sweet release of death. It would come, once half of his flesh was dissolved.

One nice final meal for the pod before its fiery end.

"Couldn't have happened to a nicer guy," Lewy remarked.

STOMP! STOMP!

Another tree came crashing down. The Ceratosaurus was close, its temper hotter than the raging fire.

"This way!" Kittner said.

They ran south to the beach.

Barely five meters were crossed before the dinosaur arrived where they had been standing. It put its nose to the ground and sniffed. Through the smell of smoke and Metwally's blood, it detected that of the runaway humans.

It turned south, got a visual of the trio, and howled a booming taunt.

For Kittner, it was the smell of seawater that was spurring him on. Before long, he arrived at the sight of a rolling surf breaking apart on a jagged shoreline.

The mutant was not far behind, forcing him to act fast.

Looking to the left, he spotted the seaplane. It was at the dock built by the Chinese company. There, Herschel was helping Costa inside.

A few remnants of the original company's operation were also nearby. A few skiffs were beached a few meters east of the dock. Near the shoreline was an ATV with a trailer. A vehicle used for the maintenance crew, it had obviously served a greater purpose for some survivors as a means to escape the initial outbreak.

The trio of survivors raced for the dock.

Kittner called to Lewy, "How long will it take to take off?"

"Just a few seconds!" Lewy replied.

Vegetation exploded behind them as the Ceratosaurus arrived at the shoreline.

"We don't have a few seconds," Kittner said.

Pain, anger, and determination resulted in a fog of clumsiness in the huge beast. Its foot touched down on a wedge-shaped rock. The reaction was akin to a parent stepping on a child's LEGO. The beast lurched, stepping on another oddly shaped rock, which shifted under its weight. An attempt to pivot and regain its footing failed miserably, ending with the dinosaur falling forward.

Kittner and the civilians reached the foot of the dock. Herschel was standing by the plane's fuselage door, waving continuously until they reached the dock. Kittner stood at the base, letting Lewy and Sadie get in the plane first.

Lewy got in the pilot's seat and looked over the instruments. Fortunately, everything was in place for him to start the ignition process.

"Just a few seconds," he said.

As Kittner had warned before, they did not have a few seconds. The Ceratosaurus was on its way over. Its feet, lips, teeth, and the tip of its horn were red with the blood of its recent victims.

Sadie and Herschel got inside the plane, the latter giving a concerned glance to his boss, who remained on the shore.

"Chief?"

Kittner, eyes and gun fixed on the approaching dinosaur, started backing towards the four-wheeler. It was obvious the Ceratosaurus would wreck the plane before it would take off, and he had no intention of failing in the final seconds. It would leave the plane alone in favor of a runaway target, as it was unaware that the winged vehicle could take flight. As far as it knew, the people inside were attempting to hide from it. The Cerato's thought process would lead it to take down Kittner, then double-back to the plane and finish the job.

Besides, it remembered him from the cave. Like with the people who revived it and held it captive, the Ceratosaurus had a score to settle.

"Get that thing in the air," Kittner said.

Herschel opened his mouth to protest, but remembered the chief had little patience for such a thing. He gave an order and expected it to be obeyed. Herschel slammed the door shut.

Kittner maintained eye contact with the mutation. It stopped near the dock and looked at the plane.

"Over here, ya big iguana!" he shouted. He hopped onto the four-wheeler and started it up.

A few shots from his rifle put the dinosaur's attention back on him.

A roar delivered its message.

Kittner's plan had worked. He put the vehicle into third gear and took off down the shoreline. The Ceratosaurus was quick to follow, the island shaking under its weight.

With the wind in his hair, Kittner needed to figure out the next part of his plan. If the Ceratosaurus killed him, he would die happy knowing the others would get to safety. With that in mind, he had no intention of meeting his end today. Not if it could be avoided. At the end of the day, he was a fighter; and fighters liked to win.

The question was how. He had one full magazine and two grenades, none of which would stop that thing. A new weapon would be required to achieve victory.

His eyes went to the water and the remains of a boat wreckage in the shallows.

Or some reinforcements.

Kittner veered to the right and took the four-wheeler into the water. The Ceratosaurus followed.

Now in three feet of water, the vehicle stalled.

Tall waves kicked up behind Kittner as the Ceratosaurus stepped into the water. Just as many others had experienced before him, a vast shadow enveloped the chief.

A last shadow.

For them. Not for Kittner.

Feeling the warmth of the creature's breath coming from above, he jumped to the left.

The creature's jaws slammed shut, imploding the four-wheeler and lifting it into the air.

With the beast momentarily distracted by its 'kill', Kittner rushed to the nearby skiff. He yanked it into the water, lifted himself over the gunwale, then knelt by the outboard. It came alive with the first yank of the ripcord. The propellers came to life and began pushing the small boat out to sea.

The Ceratosaurus spat out the vile-tasting hunk of metal that had moments before been a four-wheeler. It looked over at the skiff and bellowed, infuriated that the troublesome human had outwitted it yet again.

Just to add icing on the cake, Kittner armed a grenade and tossed it at the big lizard. It bounced off its shoulder and exploded, knocking the Ceratosaurus to the right. Shrapnel dug into the open wounds, unleashing fresh rivers of blood.

"Yeah? That piss you off?"

Kittner looked to the open ocean, hoping the grenade explosion was successful in its secondary purpose—to ring the dinner bell.

The Ceratosaurus waded into the water. Even at a twelve-foot depth, it moved remarkably fast.

Kittner let his final grenade fly. It exploded near the Cerato's leg, kicking up a large wave. The Ceratosaurus stumbled. Feeling as though it would lose its balance, it compensated by shifting its bodyweight and rotating to its right.

The huge tail made a wide swing, grazing the water's surface as it came for Kittner.

"SHIT!"

He threw himself overboard.

The tail connected with the small boat. In a heartbeat, it disappeared into a thousand pieces.

A rolling wave traveled from the point of impact, taking Kittner another ten feet out to sea. With the seafloor way below his feet, Kittner removed his vest and holster and relieved himself of the extra weight.

He breached the surface and regained his bearings.

The Ceratosaurus was already looking at him. There was an aura of confidence and satisfaction in those eyes, as if the thing knew the Chief was out of tricks. Even in the last minute, he had duped the creature twice. But now, he was struggling to stay afloat. And he could only move so fast in the water.

The Ceratosaurus knew this, and relished in the knowledge of its perceived victory.

Its sense of triumph was interrupted by a roaring sound from the docks. It looked to the west in utter bewilderment. The plane skidded over the water, then lifted into the sky, taking the other four humans far from its reach.

It roared and slapped its tail, infuriated to have been outsmarted yet again. Unfamiliar with the world of technology, it never could have guessed that the structure would have been able to take flight. Only winged animals had such a gift.

Kittner smiled.

"Feeling duped? Gotta say, big head doesn't mean you've got a big brain."

It turned its gaze back at him. All there was to do now was take solace in slaying the leader of the small group. After all, it saw no way he could outwit the large predator again.

The Ceratosaurus moved in for the kill, outstretched its jaws, and lowered its head.

A giant swell of water pushed Kittner out of the way. That swell, like a moth's cocoon, slit open. From under the crystal blue veil came a swarm of tentacles.

Like a swarm of angry eels, they crowded the dumbfounded Ceratosaurus, lassoing its neck and arms. The reptilian stumbled forward, not only caught off guard by the cephalopod's mere arrival, but its immense strength. The slimy limbs gripped it with crushing force, dwarfing the might of the mother centipede.

Any attempt to pull backward proved fruitless. The kraken had latched on and had no plans of letting go.

With flight out of the question, the Ceratosaurus resorted to fighting.

It brought its jaws down on a limb which had snared its forearm. The teeth punctured the muscular flesh, intertwining as the jaws closed tighter. A spurt of blood left the stub of the tentacle as its end was severed.

More huge waves rolled from the fight as the huge octopus revealed its horrible mass. Red in color and covered in uneven, blistering textures, the thing resembled a rotting organ more than it did an animal. But it was an animal, and a hungry one at that. One lost limb, which would quickly be regrown, would not make it back away from this fight.

Its other seven arms continued the assault.

Suction cups pulsed, revealing the serrated claws concealed within. Assisted by the intense pressure from the constricting arms, they dug into the Cerato's flesh, securing the cephalopod's grip.

The Ceratosaurus pulled back again, nearly lifting its opponent's entire mantle out of the water.

The octopus put its syphon to work, jetting itself into deeper water with the dinosaur in tow.

Even with its feet firmly planted into the seabed, the Ceratosaurus could not hold position. It skidded farther south, the water now creeping above its midsection. Two arms tightened around its neck.

Sensing its airway closed off, the creature gave in to the overwhelming anxiety engulfing its senses. All of its life, both in prehistoric and modern times, it dominated every clash it had ever taken part of. It was used to battling on dry land, its own turf. But this was in water with an opponent with a completely different biology than its own. Worse than that, this aquatic foe seemingly did not tire. If anything, its strength only enhanced with each passing moment.

Kittner backstroked, watching the incredible event unfold before his eyes. The Ceratosaurus had not given up yet. Unable to overpower the cephalopod, it decided to go all in on an assault, throwing its mass atop of the octopus.

Teeth intertwined over a section of the mantle, separating a chunk of flesh. Clouds of blood quickly expanded, the mantle appearing partially deflated following the breach.

But the sea beast was not interested in giving up. As a matter of fact, the Cerato's new strategy appeared to play into its own, as the dinosaur was not the only one with a crushing bite.

A beak, made of bone harder than titanium, extended from the center of the ring of tentacles. Parting like a pair of spring clamps, they were pressed to the dinosaur's left knee, where they pressed down on flesh and bone.

The Ceratosaurus pointed its snout at the sky and, even with its throat closed by the choking arms, howled in a fit of madness. Defiant, it lowered its head and gored the cephalopod with its horn. But the octopus refused to let up. It increased the pressure, breaking the Cerato's knee with a sound that rivaled that of a C-4 explosive.

One of those arms reached up at the dinosaur's head and coiled over its snout. The Ceratosaurus attempted to shake the limb off, but like a rodent in the grip of a python, the harder it resisted, the harder the tentacle squeezed.

Kittner kicked and paddled. His muscles ached and gravity threatened to pull him under the waves.

Every effort to swim to shore was hindered by the huge swells generated by the fight. Again and again, Kittner was swept farther away from the safety of land. Even his Navy SEAL training would only last him so long. He was a natural in the water, but even an adept swimmer like Kittner was doomed to drown if not granted a lifeline.

From the southwest came the familiar sound of a plane engine at low altitude.

He turned to his left. Coming in for a landing was the seaplane, previously intended to rescue Zahara, now operated by Lewy, who was making a Hail Mary attempt for a rescue.

Water spewed from the floats as they connected with the ocean. The large white vehicle settled forty feet from the Master Chief, its fuselage door opening to reveal a wide-eyed Herschel.

"Yeah, like we were actually going to leave you here," he shouted. "Get your ass over here, Chief!"

It was an instruction Kittner was more than happy to follow. Fueled by the catharsis brought by the return of his teammates, he quickly crossed the relatively short distance.

Herschel took his hand and pulled him aboard.

"If you ask me, there goes seven or eight of your nines, Kittner."

The Chief patted him on the shoulder. "You might be right." He looked over at Costa, who was laid across three seats. "How you holding up?"

"There was some morphine in the medical kit," Herschel explained.

"And booze in the storage compartment," Costa said, gleefully lifting a bottle of whiskey.

Kittner chuckled. "You earned it."

In the front passenger seat was Sadie. The journalist, who had come to this island in search of a story, hardly paid attention to the terrifying clash taking place in the water, but rather fixated on Lewy as he lifted the plane out of the water.

“We’re out of here,” the yacht captain-turned-pilot announced.

Kittner took a seat and enjoyed a breath of fresh air, liberated from the strains of battle.

“What happens now?” Sadie asked.

“Our associate will arrive by nightfall as expected. Knowing him, he’ll have plenty of explosives we can put to good use. When he gets here, we’ll see to it nobody gets those chemical weapons or that piece of rock.” Kittner rested his head against the back of his seat. “After that, we’re going home. And home is where I plan to stay.”

Costa raised her bottle in a toast. Herschel, sporting a small travel-sized bottle of bourbon, returned her gesture.

All things had to come to an end. Thus was the case for their time as gun-for-hires.

“Can’t imagine a better way to go out than battling resurrected dinosaurs,” Herschel remarked.

“Indeed,” Kittner said.

He looked out the window and witnessed the conclusion of the battle as the plane made distance.

The Ceratosaurus was neck-deep, the water around it red with its blood. One eye was bulging from its socket and the pressure surroundings its jaw had removed some of its teeth.

With the last of its energy, it growled and tried to pull away, but to no avail. Another tentacle wrapped over the back of its head and assisted the others in one final pull.

Sounding off a deathly snarl, the Ceratosaurus sank below the waves.

To its death.

CHECK OUT OTHER GREAT DINOSAUR THRILLERS

JURASSIC ISLAND
by Viktor Zarkov

Guided by satellite photos and modern technology a ragtag group of survivalists and scientists travel to an uncharted island in the remote South Indian Ocean. Things go to hell in a hurry once the team reaches the island and the massive megalodon that attacked their boats is only the beginning of their desperate fight for survival.

Nothing could have prepared billionaire explorer Joseph Thornton and washed up archaeologist Christopher "Colt" McKinnon for the terrifying prehistoric creatures that wait for them on JURASSIC ISLAND!

K-REX
by L.Z. Hunter

Deep within the Congo jungle, Circuitz Mining employs mercenaries as security for its Coltan mining site. Armed with assault rifles and decades of experience, nothing should go wrong. However, the dangers within the jungle stretch beyond venomous snakes and poisonous spiders. There is more to fear than guerrillas and vicious animals. Undetected, something lurks under the expansive treetop canopy . . .

Something ancient.

Something dangerous.

Kasai Rex!

CHECK OUT OTHER GREAT DINOSAUR THRILLERS

SPINOSAURUS
by Hugo Navikov

Brett Russell is a hunter of the rarest game. His targets are cryptids, animals denied by science. But they are well known by those living on the edges of civilization, where monsters attack and devour their animals and children and lay ruin to their shantytowns.
When a shadowy organization sends Brett to the Congo in search of the legendary dinosaur cryptid Kasai Rex, he will face much more than a terrifying monster from the past.
Spinosaurus is a dinosaur thriller packed with intrigue, action and giant prehistoric predators.

LAND OF DEATH
by Eric S Brown & Alex Laybourne

A group of American soldiers, fleeing an organized attack on their base camp in the Middle East, encounter a storm unlike anything they've seen before. When the storm subsides, they wake up to find themselves no longer in the desert and perhaps not even on Earth. The jungle they've been deposited in is a place ruled by prehistoric creatures long extinct. Each day is a struggle to survive as their ammo begins to run low and virtually everything they encounter, in this land they've been hurled into, is a deadly threat.

SEVEREDPRESS

facebook.com/severedpress
twitter.com/severedpress

CHECK OUT OTHER GREAT DINOSAUR THRILLERS

WRITTEN IN STONE
by David Rhodes

Charles Dawson is trapped 100 million years in the past. Trying to survive from day to day in a world of dinosaurs he devises a plan to change his fate. As he begins to write messages in the soft mud of a nearby stream, he can only hope they will be found by someone who can stop his time travel. Professor Ron Fontana and Professor Ray Taggit, scientists with opposing views, each discover the fossilized messages. While attempting to save Charles, Professor Fontana, his daughter Lauren and their friend Danny are forced to join Taggit and his group of mercenaries. Taggit does not intend to rescue Charles Dawson, but to force Dawson to travel back in time to gather samples for Taggit's fame and fortune. As the two groups jump through time they find they must work together to make it back alive as this fast-paced thriller climaxes at the very moment the age of dinosaurs is ending.

HARD TIME
by Alex Laybourne

Rookie officer Peter Malone and his heavily armed team are sent on a deadly mission to extract a dangerous criminal from a classified prison world. A Kruger Correctional facility where only the hardest, most vicious criminals are sent to fend for themselves, never to return.

But when the team come face to face with ancient beasts from a lost world, their mission is changed. The new objective: Survive.

Printed in Dunstable, United Kingdom

78854718R00097